Keeping Secrets

Book Three in the Boone Series

by Jim Hartsell

House Mountain Publishing

Cover design by:
www.nickcastledesign.com

ISBN 978-1-7327549-2-8

Also by Jim Hartsell

The Boone Series:

Pushing Back (Book One)
Matching Scars (Book Two)

Other Fiction:

Tango
Rock, Paper, Scissors
Journey

Children's Books:

The Box of Toys
Father and Sister Radish and the
        Rose-Colored Glasses
The Mountain Climber

Non-Fiction:

Glimpses
Sisyphus and the Itsy-Bitsy Spider

Chapter One

"Where's Frankie?"

"She's right here, Mr. Connell," I say for the third time. I'm holding Frankie's collar and we're standing about a foot away from him. He doesn't answer me and then I say, "If you stick your hand out you can touch her, she's sitting next to your chair."

Mr. Connell doesn't say anything for a half a minute, and then he says, "Where's Frankie?"

Sometimes I feel sorry for the old man, but today he's just pissing me off something awful. I'm trying to decide whether or not to just go on to somebody else when Frankie scoots a little closer, so she's almost in his lap, and touches her nose to his hand.

He jerks a little and then, like he's figured out what just touched him, kind of moves his hand around and finally gets it on Frankie's head. He's still looking straight out in front of him, but once he gets his hand on her head he settles down some and he sort of halfway scratches at her ear.

I stand there not saying anything. The last two or three times I tried to talk to Mr. Connell it didn't go anywhere. I'd say something and he'd either repeat it right back to me or say something that didn't make any sense. So I don't try anymore.

After about a minute or two his hand kind of goes limp and Frankie scoots back toward me. I'm thinking that means I can go on, so I say, "We'll see you later, Mr. Connell."

No answer.

I let go of Frankie's collar and take a couple of steps. The leash tightens up and Frankie looks at me and then gets up and turns away from Mr. Connell.

"C'mon, girl," I say, and we head off across the sidewalk and around the fountain. Betty is walking out of the main building and heads toward me.

"You were just with Mr. Connell, weren't you?" she's bending down and scratching Frankie behind her left ear.

"Yeah, he barely knew we were there."

She straightens up. "I know. I'm getting worried about him. He's got more and more of that kind of day." She looks over at him and then back at me. "Is he the first one you've seen today?"

I nod. "I was thinking I'd try one or two more. I know it's close to lunch."

"You don't eat at the cafeteria much, Boone. Don't you like our food?"

I start to tell her she doesn't need to be keeping track of how much I eat like she's my momma and then I realize she's just teasing me.

"The food's okay, Betty, but the waiter got my order wrong the last time."

Betty laughs out loud. "Well, we'll just have to speak to the staff, Boone."

I know about waiters and stuff like that because since I moved into that little house at the back of the property I've been watching TV again. Truth is, I've never really been waited on, because I've never been to a fancy restaurant.

Wonder if Nancy would like to go get something to eat sometime. We ate at Gamaliel's house a few times when I was living there, but that was just sandwiches and spaghetti and frozen pizza and stuff like that, and I don't really like to eat at her house because of her daddy Stan.

"So what's for lunch today?" I ask Betty; she's walking with me. I'm headed toward Mrs. Reston and Betty's going somewhere in that same direction, I guess.

"You know, I'm not sure," she says. "What is today, Tuesday?"

I shrug. What day it is doesn't mean too much to me.

"If it's Tuesday, it might be chicken. They serve chicken a lot on Tuesdays."

7

I turn toward Mrs. Reston and Betty keeps going straight. Mrs. Reston is standing under a big old hickory tree staring out at the parking lot.

"Hi, Mrs. Reston."

I know what's coming next. The same thing that always comes next.

"Young man, why are you not in school?"

"You know, Mrs. Reston, I'm finished with school, remember?"

So far that's been enough. She's never asked me if I've graduated, and I'm sure not going to tell her I didn't. When I say I'm finished with school, that's the truth, and it seems like it satisfies her.

"Do you see a green station wagon out there anywhere, young man?"

She points toward the parking lot and I look. No green cars at all.

"Sorry, Mrs. Reston, I don't see one. You expecting somebody?"

"My granddaughter. She's been over in Europe for the last three years, and my son called and said she's back and wants to see me."

I need to ask Betty or Mark what I'm supposed to do when this kind of thing happens. Mrs. Reston doesn't have a son. She doesn't have any children at all. Not unless she's been keeping that a secret from everybody here.

Since I don't know what to do, I say, "You want to help me take Frankie for a walk?"

Mrs. Reston turns to me and gives me a sad little smile. "I don't think so. I think I'll just wait here until Rosemary gets here."

"Okay," I say. "Maybe tomorrow or sometime."

She nods but I can tell she's not listening.

Chicken doesn't sound all that good so I head back to the house with Frankie and get the leftover pizza out of the fridge. I eat it cold with an S&S to wash it down, and I'm finishing off the last of it when there's a knock on the door.

Frankie is up and facing the door. She's not growling, so that's good. The first thing I do is look in the kitchen to make sure I put the jar of shine back with the others. It's right out there on the counter, so I get up quiet and put it in the cabinet. When I go back into the living room I pass by the closet and think about the shotgun, but I leave it in there.

I'm about to decide whether to open the door or not when the knob starts turning. I never lock my door, so it's swinging open before I can get across the room to put my foot against it.

The door swings open wide and Maryanne is standing there. She takes one step in and stops when she sees me. When she sees Frankie she jumps backward, reaches back in, grabs the knob and slams the door shut.

I say, "Stay here a minute, Frankie," and walk across the room, which only takes about three steps. When I open the door she's ten feet away and walking fast toward the main building. When I close the door behind me she stops and turns around.

"I am so sorry, Mr. Boone, I thought you were talking to the people, like you do after lunch."

"I did that before lunch today," I say. "You were just going to walk on in?"

The thing about where I used to live, in Gamaliel's house, was when somebody came in without asking it was usually Jerry. Now that I think about it, I guess she's lucky I wasn't pointing the shotgun at her when she swung the door open. I start to tell her that but she's already talking.

"Miss Betty, she told me that your house was one of the places I was supposed to keep up, you know, like I do all the rooms." She points to the ground beside her and there's one of those big plastic baskets with handles and it's got towels and toilet paper and spray bottles and stuff like that in it. "She asked me yesterday if I had been keeping your house clean and I said I didn't know I was supposed to. She got kind of mad and said I had to start right away, that I should have been doing that all along. I'm sorry, Mr. Boone, I didn't know I was supposed to look after your place."

Last time I saw one of those plastic baskets it was just sitting in the hallway outside Mr. Abernathy's room and I was almost out of toilet paper and I just took two of the rolls. There were still two left and I didn't think anything about it. Towels and stuff like that, I've just been using them and they get dry in between times and I don't worry about it.

Thinking about people just coming in and out of my house pisses me off a little. For one thing, there's the shine I've got in the cabinet. Then there's the two guns in the closet. I guess that's about it, but still, just walking in like that, it's not right. When I was living with Momma and Daddy and Hannah, and Frankie before he died, the only one that came around was Mr. Wilcox, cause he owned the property, and I remember him and Daddy in the yard next to Mr. Wilcox's big dually and Daddy was right up in his face. I thought Mr. Wilcox was going to take a swing at him, but Daddy was pretty scary when he got like that, and so they just shouted at each other for a while and then he got in that big truck and drove off. I thought sure he was going to throw us out of the house, but he didn't. Maybe he needed the workers and maybe he felt sorry for Momma and Hannah. I don't know.

Anyway, we never had anybody just come in like Maryanne was about to do.

I take a step toward her. She doesn't back up, but she looks like she wants to.

"So you've never been in there before?"

She's shaking her head. "No, Mr. Boone, this was going to be my first day. I'm good at my job, and I won't bother anything. Just cleaning."

"I don't like people poking around my stuff."

"No poking, I promise. I've got these towels and paper and I just come in and clean the place up. It looks like a small place. I won't take long, and I won't mess up anything."

"Okay, then, come on in." I want to see what all she's going to do.

"You mean now?"

I nod. "A minute ago you were going to clean up."

She doesn't move, and finally I say, "Frankie's a good dog. She knows about people. Come on in and I'll show you."

She's really scared of Frankie, I can tell. I wonder if that means she's an asshole like Jerry is. She doesn't seem like Jerry, not even close, and Frankie didn't growl or anything when she was at the door. I decide to tell her that, see if it helps.

"Look, Frankie knew you were at the door and she didn't growl or bark or anything. She must think you're okay. Come on in and say hi to her."

Maryanne just stands there.

"Okay, I'll bring her out here." I can see by the look on her face she doesn't like that idea at all.

"Look, Maryanne, you've got to get used to her sooner or later. She lives here now, and if you're going to be coming into my house, she might be here sometime when I'm not."

That last part's not really true. Frankie goes pretty much everywhere with me. I decide I'm going to try one more time and then the hell with it.

"I'll bring Frankie out here and I'll hang on to her collar. She's not going to hurt you, not with me right here."

Wonder why she's so scared of Frankie. Maybe she's just scared of dogs in general. I don't get that at all. Frankie's great, and most of the dogs I've been around have been too. Johnson, one of Tiny's friends, has a big pit bull that he's trained up to be mean, and I don't want anything to do with that dog. Pretty much every other dog, though, is okay with me.

She's still standing there, so I go back inside and get Frankie. When I get back outside, she's still there but I swear she's shaking like a leaf. For a second I think about turning Frankie loose just to see what would happen, but I don't do that. I walk over real slow with my hand wrapped around Frankie's collar.

I'm standing there right in front of Maryanne with Frankie beside me and she's staring at Frankie and trying hard to stop shaking. Frankie is sniffing the air, tail wagging a little, and then the hair on her neck bristles and she starts growling low down so Maryanne and I can barely hear her.

Maryanne's really scared now and I'm wondering what the hell is going on here. One minute she's all friendly and the next it's like she's about to jump Maryanne. I look at Maryanne and there are tears starting down her face and she takes a step backward and I'm trying to figure out whether to say something to her or to Frankie.

She takes another step back and when I look up past her I see somebody standing at the corner of the main building.

It's Jerry.

Chapter Two

I know if I let Frankie go she'll take off toward him and Maryanne might have a heart attack right there, thinking Frankie's after her, but there's part of me that wants to turn her loose.

Maryanne sees me looking past her and turns around. I can tell she doesn't want to because that puts Frankie behind her but she does it anyway. So we're all three standing there just staring at that shithead and me wondering why he's here. My dog is straining at her collar and I'm still thinking about letting her go to see what happens.

Just about the time I open my mouth to say something, Jerry turns around and disappears behind the corner of the main building. Maryanne turns back to me.

"That was Mr. Jerry, wasn't it?"

I nod and then say, "Why do you call everybody Mr.?"

"What?"

"I said, why do you call everybody Mr.? Like me, I'm your age or maybe younger than you are, and you call me Mr. Boone. Why do you do that?"

She doesn't answer right away and I say, "Forget it. It's just weird, is all. Yeah, that was Jerry. Wonder what that piece of shit is doing here. Gamaliel's gone, how come he's sneaking around like that?"

Right away I think about the money. I know Gamaliel didn't tell him about it, or he'd have been all over me before the old guy was even in the ground. And then I think, he's not in the ground, he's in that jar sitting on a table somewhere, and I start laughing. I can't stop myself.

Maryanne looks at me like I'm crazy and I wave my hand at her and say, "Never mind. Here, hold Frankie while I go get her leash."

I take one step and I'm right next to her. I grab her by the wrist and slip her hand under Frankie's collar. "Don't let go or she'll take off after Jerry. I'll be right back."

Now she's shaking all over again, but I don't give her a chance to say anything. I just do it and then turn around and head into the house. I figure I can trust Frankie not to drag her all over the place.

It only takes a second and I'm back and snap on the leash. "C'mon, Frankie, let's go see Betty or Mark. Wonder if they even know he was on the property."

Maryanne is standing there, still holding on to Frankie, and I say, "Remember, no poking around. I'll be back in a minute."

She shakes her head and looks down at Frankie. "She's a really nice dog, isn't she?"

I nod. "I think she likes you."

She tries to smile and I say, "Frankie, let's go find Betty."

Halfway to the building I turn and look back and she's carrying the plastic basket toward the front door.

We can't find Betty or Mark; a lot of the old folks are in their rooms taking a nap, and Jerry is nowhere to be seen. I go up to Diana, one of the people who works with the ones that are really bad off, that have to be pushed around and fed and have their asses wiped and all that shit. I don't know how anybody does that; before Gamaliel died I thought about having him back in his house with me taking care of him and that thinking lasted about a minute, until I thought about what I'd have to do. I guess Diana likes it, though, cause she's always happy and smiling and talking to these old people that can't even do more than grunt at you. I couldn't do it.

Diana looks up from wiping some drool off of Mrs. Caughorn's chin. "Hi, Boone! Hi, Frankie! How are you two this fine day?"

She's like that all the damn time.

"Hey, Diana, did you see Jerry just now? You know, Gamaliel's son-in-law?"

She shakes her head. "Me and Mrs. Caughorn, we just rolled out the door a second ago, looking for a sunny spot to sit in. Isn't that right, dear?"

Mrs. Caughorn is one of those that I've just about given up trying to talk to. Even Frankie can't get through.

"Okay, thanks." I turn to go and then turn back. "Bye, Mrs. Caughorn."

"Did you hear that, sweetie? Boone is saying goodbye. Can you give him a little smile?" Diana never gives up, even when she probably ought to.

Mrs. Caughorn just sits there.

Frankie and I go on around the building and there's no Jerry and nobody else to ask about him.

When we get back to the little house, Maryanne is coming out the front door.

"No luck finding Jerry," I say. "You done already?"

She nods. "All I do is give you new towels and paper and clean up the sink and shower. And the toilet. I don't do anything in the rest of the house."

Okay, I think. No way she can find anything I don't want her to see if that's really all she does.

"Well, thanks."

She smiles. "You're welcome, Mr. Boone. I'll be back in a week." She looks down at Frankie but

18

doesn't reach out or anything. "Frankie really is a pretty dog, isn't she?"

"You hear that, Frankie?" I say, rubbing her side. "This lady thinks you're pretty."

Frankie is eating this up, and I think for a second that Maryanne is going to pet her, but she's still not doing that.

"I have to go, Mr. Boone, I don't want to fall behind and stay late. Stephen always picks me up at 5:30."

I don't know who Stephen is, and don't ask. Probably a boyfriend or somebody in her family. I look at her hand and she's not wearing a ring or anything. Wonder why she doesn't drive herself.

"Okay, see ya. And why don't you stop calling me Mr.? Sounds like you're talking to some old guy."

"I don't know, Mr. Boone. I do this for everybody here."

She picks up her basket and heads toward the main building.

Chapter Three

"Would you be more comfortable meeting at your place?" Mark is sitting behind his desk and I'm in one of the two chairs on the other side. Frankie is over in the corner about half asleep.

He's talking about the living room in that little house on the back of the property. Not my place, really, and doesn't seem right for him to call it that. I can't tell whether he's making fun of me or not.

It doesn't bother me, not having a place. I never have had one, just moved from one house to another. This one and Gamaliel's have been the best, no cracks in the floor or leaky windows or roofs, so I'm warm and dry and that's better than some places I've been in. Still it's not mine.

"No, this is okay, but next time, if it's not raining, let's go sit out under the big tree next to the chapel."

He smiles. "That's a great idea, Boone. We'll get some sweet tea and something to snack on from the kitchen." He looks out the window. "After this storm, we'll have to clean off the picnic table and chairs, though."

The wind is whipping around the side of the building and the trees are swaying. Rain hasn't really started yet, but it's supposed to be a bad one.

"Okay, you said you had some new stories for me." Mark gets out a pencil and some paper. "Who was it you were talking to again?"

"Mr. Vande— Vander— what the hell is his name, anyway? The new guy."

"Vandergriff. Eliot Vandergriff."

"Yeah, him. Man loves to talk. I think he would've gone on for an hour or two if they hadn't come to get him for some appointment."

Mark grins. "I had the same experience with his son when they came to get the grand tour."

"Well, the first story is about his daddy. World War I. You want to hear that one or just stuff about him?"

"Boone, the whole point of this is to keep these stories from fading away. Anything you've got I'd love to hear. We, I mean I'll, sort it out later. Don't even worry about whether or not it's true."

"Okay."

He leans forward and puts his elbows on the desk. "Whenever you're ready."

"Okay. His dad's name was Heyard. He — "

"Wait a minute. You sure about that name?"

"Not real sure, no. Could have been something else."

"Howard, maybe? I'll look it up. Keep going."

"Okay. Heyard or whatever his name is, he grew up poor, around here somewhere, sounded like close to Kentucky maybe. He was the second youngest and everybody else older than him was gone across the state line to the coal mines or off to the Army, except his sister, he only had one, and she married a coal miner and already had a kid on the way. This was 1917, early 1918 maybe. Heyard was just turned seventeen, according to Eliot, but he was pretty big for his age, and he wanted out awful bad. They'd get letters from the older boys, them that was already in the army, about what they had to eat and getting brand new uniforms and all that, and Heyard was eating beans and cornbread eight or ten times a week, and clothes falling off of him. So he wanted in.

"Eliot says that his daddy just kept after his parents, Eliot's grandparents, until he just wore them down and they finally told him to go on and see if he could get in."

When I finish telling Mark about how Heyard got in, got through boot camp, and was on the boat headed for Europe when the war ended, Mark nods and says, "Okay, that's good. Anything from Eliot? Any stories about him yet?"

"He started in on one, but his version of his daddy's story, the one I just told you, went on for so long that he didn't do much more than get his next story started when they came to get him."

"He'll finish it the next time, I guess."

"Probably pick up right where he left off. He's got a good memory, far as I can tell."

Mark doesn't say anything for a minute and I say, "Listen, I was looking for you the other day, wanted to ask you something."

He studies me for a second. "Everything all right, Boone?"

"Yeah. Well, I don't know for sure. I'm pretty sure I saw Jerry the other day, but by the time I got up to the building he wasn't anywhere around, didn't see him in the parking lot, and you and Betty weren't out anywhere."

"Jerry? Gamaliel's son-in-law?"

I nod.

"What's he doing here?"

"I don't know, Mark, that's why I was looking for you and Betty. I don't know that he's got any business being on this property, so it didn't seem right that he was just out there wandering around."

"I remember from Gamaliel's service the look he was giving you. He doesn't like you much, I take it."

I'm trying real hard not to call Jerry an asshole here in Mark's office, him being a preacher and all, so

I start out saying, "I feel that way about him, too, the way he treated me and Carrie. That asshole — sorry, Mark."

He laughs a little. "I could tell you were kind of stumbling around. Don't worry about it. You can make it up to me by starting to come to Sunday service."

I get all mad and start to tell him to stay out of my business and then I look at him and realize he's teasing me.

He grins. "Gotcha."

I can't help but smile back, but it doesn't last. Now that I've started thinking about Jerry I can't stop, seems like.

"So you don't have any idea why he might be coming back around. I swear, Mark, when I saw him he was just standing there staring at me. I thought about turning Frankie loose but I don't trust that son of a bitch — sorry, Mark."

Mark looks at me and shakes his head. "You must really hate that guy. Careful; there's no good end to that road."

I really can't stand it when he talks like a preacher, but I guess I asked for that one.

Three days later there's another knock on the door and Nancy says, "Boone? Are you home?"

Frankie's up and wagging all over. I try to think; it's only been a couple of weeks since we saw Nancy, but Frankie's acting like she's been gone a month.

When I open the door she's standing there with a big grocery bag in her hand. She puts it down and throws her arms around me and gives me a long kiss.

"Happy birthday!"

I step back and just look at her for a second, and then I say, "How did you know when my birthday was?"

"I looked on your driver's license, you know, when we were at the bank that first time. You had to show him some I.D. and when he handed it back I took it from him before you had a chance to. You're 18 now, Boone! Happy birthday!"

She's smiling and I look at her and say, "What's in the bag?"

Right away she stops smiling. "Just some peach pie I made about an hour ago. I've got some ice cream right here . . . ." She stops when she sees the look on my face.

"What's the matter, Boone?"

"You shouldn't have done that, Nancy."

"Done what?"

All I can think of right now is that time when Momma made that peach pie even though nobody had died and we had pie and ice cream and it was so great and then Daddy came home all drunk and mean and threw the pie out into the yard. I tell myself she doesn't know about that time, no way she could have known that it was a peach pie, but it doesn't matter.

And she doesn't know that we never did shit for my birthday or anybody else's in the family, not ever. Momma tried a few times, made us something special for supper or some little present, but she had to make sure Daddy didn't find out about it. He'd get mad and start screaming at her about wasted time and money and how it was no big deal that I was a year older. It just meant I needed to get off my ass and go get a job. First time he said that I was twelve. So I got no good memories of birthdays or pies or anything like that.

All I can think of right now is I need to be by myself.

"You better go on home now."

The look on her face is so sad, she looks like she's about to cry, and I don't care, I just want her to go away.

"I don't understand, Boone, what's wrong? What did I do wrong? I thought we could, we could, you know, just have some pie and ice cream and you could open your — "

"I said you go on home now!" I'm shouting at her and now she is crying, and Frankie is still standing there wagging her tail but she's figuring out something is bad wrong.

I slam the door and I can hear her outside and now she's crying hard, and I know I ought to open up the door and start apologizing to her right now but I just can't make myself do it.

Finally I shout at the closed door. "You don't know! You don't understand! You — "

There's no noise from the other side.

Then I hear somebody step up on the little porch and I grab the door and pull it open and say, "Hey, I'm sor — "

Betty is standing there.

"What did you do to that poor girl, Boone? I was out in the parking lot and she came running up, just bawling, and opened her car door and threw some bags in and got in and slammed the door. She's out there bawling her eyes out right now. What did you say to her?"

I don't think I've ever seen Betty this mad before.

She's still talking. "If you were getting ready to say I'm sorry you're saying it to the wrong person. You better get your ass out there right now. She's a good girl, Boone, you need to make this right."

"I can't, Betty, it's too late."

She's shaking her head. "No, it's not, but before long it will be. I've seen you two together, I know how you feel about her. You better get going."

I just stand there like a fool.

Betty turns around and starts back. She says over her shoulder, "You're a fool if you let her go, Boone. That girl, she, well . . . you better not let her go, is all I can say."

I don't know how, I don't know how to fix this, and all I can see is that damn peach pie in the middle of the yard and Momma crying and Daddy yelling at her to shut the hell up.

I'm looking at the floor and when I look up Betty's gone. Frankie is standing right beside me, nuzzling my hand. I don't even have the energy to pet her. She starts off the porch and looks back at me like, "C'mon, Boone, let's go find her."

My damn dog's smarter than I am.

I go out the front door and take a few steps and then think, the hell with it, I'm too late anyway, and I go back inside. There's nothing in the fridge to eat and I don't care, not really hungry anyway. I start to make an S&S and look at the jar. It's only about a third full, so I just take it into the living room and sit down on the couch.

Frankie comes over and sits on the floor next to me. I look at her and say, "Girl, you ought to go find somebody else to live with. You're hanging out with a real loser."

She pushes her head up under my hand and lays her muzzle on my leg. I start to push her off or shout at her to get the hell away from me, but I don't even have the energy to do that. I take another sip and wonder what Nancy's doing right now.

Chapter Four

Mark's sitting under the big tree close to the chapel when Frankie and I come out the side door.

It's been a week since I ran Nancy off and I don't have any new stories for Mark. Truth is, I haven't left the house more than a couple of times and one of those was to go to the store to pick up some Thunderstorm and some frozen shit to eat. I started to call Nancy at least three times and never did. I don't know what I would say even if she would talk to me.

I come up to the empty chair and sit down, and Mark just sits there for a long time looking right at me. It's starting to piss me off and I'm about to just get up and leave when he says, "So, you ready to tell me what's eating you up inside?"

I'm about to tell him to mind his own damn business but when I open my mouth it all starts pouring out, all about how Nancy came over and had peach pie and ice cream and a birthday present and how I slammed the door in her face and how I really screwed things up this time and what a sorry piece of shit I am and Mark holds up his hand.

"Slow down, Boone, just slow down a second."

I take a deep breath and then I'm right back into it, not slowing down at all, and I tell Mark all about when I was a kid and about the peach pie that Momma made and how Daddy threw it in the yard. I'm right next to crying by now, and Mark jumps in the next time I stop to take another breath.

"Boone, does Nancy know any of this?"

I shake my head no.

"Well, don't you think you ought to tell her?"

"Mark, there's no way she's going to talk to me. I was a real shit. Just like my daddy would've done."

"I think you need to try, Boone. What could it hurt? You say you've already messed things up."

I don't know why I just did that, tell Mark about Daddy and all. That's nobody's business but mine and Momma and Hannah. Everybody else that was there is dead. I stand up quick, while Mark is still talking.

"I gotta go, Mark."

Mark looks up at me. "You can stay, you know. As long as you want to. Sounds like you've got some stuff you need to get off your chest. You know, I'm a preacher. Anything you talk to me about, I won't tell anybody. Can't, actually. So if you want to talk about

Nancy, or your father, or when you were growing up, you just let me know."

Now I really have to get out of here. There's no way he knows about Daddy, I tell myself, but what he's saying still scares me.

I turn and say, "C'mon, Frankie, let's get out of here."

We're a couple of steps away when Mark says, "I'll pray for you, Boone."

"Just like a damn preacher," I say to Frankie. "Next thing you know he'll be asking for an offering."

I'm really mad now, mad at Mark and Nancy and Daddy and Momma, Momma most of all for taking off like that and leaving both of us. Well, she didn't really leave Hannah, she got Aunt Claire to take her in. She just left me. Why did she do that? Looks like Nancy's leaving me, too. I keep walking and talking, sometimes to myself and sometimes to Frankie.

When I get to my house, Maryanne is coming out the door. She smiles and waves and I don't smile back. I don't feel like talking to anybody right now.

She bends down to pat Frankie on the head and Frankie's loving this, but I say, "Don't touch her."

Maryanne looks surprised. "Why, Mr. Boone? I thought you wanted me to get used to — "

"And stop calling me Mr. Boone. It's like I'm one of these old farts around here."

She's gathering up her stuff now, like she can't wait to get out of here. "Okay, Mr. — sorry, sorry."

She takes off toward the main building but turns and heads around to where the chapel is. Mark is still there, standing out under the tree, and she goes right up to him.

Great, I think. Now she's going to blab to him all about what a jerk I am. I go inside and almost slam the door on Frankie, but she scoots in and goes straight to her blanket.

I flip through the TV channels and then turn it off. I don't want to be here in this little house, but I can't go where I want to go.

I want to be back up at the pool, watching that big fish laze around the deep part. I want to hear nothing but the woods around me.

Or I want to be in Gamaliel's house, back in that sunroom, sitting with him and sipping and talking about nothing at all, letting the hours slip on by.

Before too long I've switched over from mad to sad, and I'm laying back on the couch staring at the ceiling thinking about how pretty much everybody else has got it better than me when the phone rings.

I almost let it go, but I make myself get up and answer it, kind of hoping it's Nancy, although I don't guess she'll be calling me or coming by again.

It's Tiny.

"Hey, man, you busy?"

"You know I'm hardly ever busy, Tiny, but if you need somebody to clean trash out of one of your buildings, you probably called the wrong guy. Seems like last time I got stuck back in the back where the shit was about knee deep."

Tiny laughs. "Why do you think I asked you to help me? Otherwise it would've been me back in there."

It's hard to stay in a bad mood around Tiny. His family's got all kinds of money, but he doesn't act like a spoiled rich kid, rubbing my nose in it all the time.

"So, what's going on?" I say, grinning in spite of myself.

"I was just wondering if you might want to take Frankie for a run tomorrow. I got a new dog the other day and he needs somebody to run with."

"So what the hell kind of dog is that?"

We're at Tiny's house, out in the back, and Frankie and the new dog are getting to know each other, sniffing butts and stuff like that. We're leaning against Daddy's piece of shit truck watching them.

"Well, I'm not exactly sure. He's from the shelter, and they say there's definitely some Lab in there, but they're not sure what else."

"You said he? Looks to me like you had his balls cut off."

Tiny sighs and says, "Shelter policy. My dog's a eunuch."

I turn to him and say, "What did you say?"

"I said eunuch. My dog's a eunuch."

"Now that sounds like some kind of made up word."

"No, it's real."

"Okay, then, what does it mean?"

"Well, back in the old days, over in the Middle East, sultans, you know, the guys running things, used to have a bunch of women who just sat around waiting on them to call them into their bedroom. They didn't want the guards that watched the women to get any ideas, so they cut their balls off and made eunuchs out of them."

I'm feeling a little sick to my stomach. "Man, that has got to be bullshit. Where did you hear that?"

"School, man. You should've paid more attention."

"Well, if that's the kind of shit they talk about, I'm glad I got out when I did."

Tiny laughs that short laugh of his. "You ready to take Frankie and Eunuch for a run?"

"That's his name?"

He nods. "Just now decided."

I shake my head. "Man, that's cold."

He shrugs. "Fits, doesn't it?"

I push myself off the truck fender and we head out, more or less toward the still.

Frankie and Eunuch are running circles around me and Tiny, wearing each other out, when Tiny stops and I walk about three more steps before I realize it and stop, too. I turn around and he's standing there, staring at me.

"So what happened with you and Nancy?" he says.

"Nothing."

"C'mon, man, I thought we were friends. What happened?"

"What makes you think anything happened?" I like Tiny, and he's helped me out a bunch, probably saved my life with that asshole Jerry, but right now he's being awful nosy. Frankie and Eunuch come over and collapse on the ground, tongues out, panting hard. For a second that's the only noise, that and a little wind in the trees up ahead.

Tiny steps up to me and looks me in the eye, then turns and watches the treetops swaying back and forth. "I ran into her yesterday down at the grocery store and asked her how you were doing. I thought she was going to bust out crying right there in the parking lot. She didn't even answer me, just turned and kind of half-ran back to her car and took off." He turns back to face me again. "That's what makes me thing something's wrong. Now if you tell me to back off, I'll do it, but I figure I had the right to ask, since we had that thing with Jerry a while back."

I don't say anything for a minute, then, "Yeah, I think I'd like you to back off."

Tiny shakes his head. "Don't screw this up, man. She's a fine girl and she's crazy about you. Whatever it is, you work it out. Now that's it. I'm backing off."

He starts walking again and the dogs are up and looking back and forth between me and Tiny.

I take a few fast steps to catch up and say, "Everything going okay up at the still?"

He grins a little. "Wait and see."

When we turn the corner around the big rock I can't believe it. The still is gone.

The big rock is there, the clearing is there, and I'm looking around and when I turn far enough to see Tiny he's trying hard not to laugh out loud. Then he points at Frankie. "Your dog's smarter than you are, man."

She's sniffing around something laying on the ground and I go over close to it and see that it's some kind of netting. When I pick it up, the whole section of brush moves along with it and I can see part of a metal bucket underneath. I let it drop back and turn around and walk six or seven steps away. I turn back and I'll be damned if it's not vanished. Then I start really looking and I can see a rough outline of about the right size for the still.

"I was thinking about doing some hunting when the season rolls around and thinking about blinds and how I've always been pretty good at building a deer blind that you, or a deer, would walk right past and never see." Tiny's pretty proud of his work, and I can see why.

He keeps going. "So, I was thinking about that and got started thinking about what we've got going up here and I decided that it just made sense for us to make it harder to see if you're just passing through."

"Tiny, you're a damned genius," I say, and mean every word of it. Unless you looked hard you'd never know anything besides brush was there.

"Don't you ever forget it, Boone," he says. "Hear that, Eunuch? You belong to a damn genius."

I guess Eunuch already knows his name, because he comes running up to Tiny and starts bouncing on his front legs. I feel kind of bad for the dog, not having any balls anymore, and that makes me wonder about Frankie.

"Hey, Tiny, do you think I need to get Frankie, you know," I'm trying to think of the word the vet used, "spayed?"

He's hunkered down scratching Eunuch behind the ears and doesn't answer for a minute.

"Yes, you're a good dog, aren't you, Eunuch? You didn't need them anyway, did you? What a good dog!"

He stops talking to Eunuch and stands back up.

"Probably. Even where you're living now, when she goes into heat there'll be dogs coming in from all over, all of them trying to climb on. And out here in the woods, you never can tell what will happen. She might get all caught up in it and take off, and you'd never see her again."

That settles it right there.

Chapter Five

Turns out getting her spayed isn't that big a deal, at least for me. Since they pay me a little at the home, I can afford it without getting into Gamaliel's money, and a week after I pick her up from the vet's I can't tell anything has been done to her.

Neither Betty or Mark has said anything about Nancy. It's been a few weeks now since I acted like such a shit, and I haven't heard from her or seen her. Maryanne is still coming down to the house once a week or so, but she doesn't do more than smile and nod, and it's not a friendly smile. It's more like I work here and I'm supposed to be nice to you smile. I feel like I should make a list of all the people I need to tell I'm sorry.

I don't like thinking about that stuff, so I spend my time either with Tiny and Eunuch or with the old folks that I'm supposed to be talking to anyway. They don't know what a jerk I am, and some of them wouldn't remember the next day even if I told them.

Eliot Vandergriff, now, he would remember. And he'd probably tell anybody who would listen, too. That man loves to talk. Last few times he's been telling me all about the Great Depression and how poor his family was and how they had to eat beans all the time and potato soup and how they didn't have any new clothes.

Sounds pretty familiar to me, but I don't say so. I've seen enough people like him to know that if I told a story he'd have to tell a better one even if it was a lie. No reason to even get started on that stuff. I listen and nod and try to remember it all so when I see Mark the next time I can tell him about it.

When I get there this time, Mark's already waiting for me. Last few meetings with him have all started the same way, and this one's no different.

"Talked to Nancy yet?"

I shake my head.

Usually the next question is, "Want me to talk to her for you?" I always shake my head no to that one too.

This time is different.

"She called me yesterday," he says. "I wasn't in the office and so far I haven't returned her call, but I'll be doing that later on today."

Why the hell didn't she call me? As soon as I ask myself that question I know the answer. She's afraid she'll get yelled at.

41

I look up and Mark's studying me from across the table. We're outside again, and, like usual, he's got a pitcher of sweet tea and a plate of sandwiches. Looks like ham this time. I look at him for just a second and then away toward the mountains off in the distance. I know I'm supposed to say something, but I'll be damned if I know what that is.

"Here's what I want to tell her," he starts out. "If you're okay with it, that is. You know anything you told me is private between you and me as long as I'm acting as a preacher."

I jump in before he can say anything else. "Don't tell her anything, then."

He frowns. "I have to tell you, Boone, I think that's a mistake. You can't tell me not to call her, and if she asks about you and I tell her that you said not to tell her anything about what's going on with you, it'll make things worse. I can almost guarantee that."

I don't say anything to that, but I know he's right. I hate this; seems like everything I think to do only makes things worse.

"Anyway," he goes on, "here's what I want to tell her. That you had a really bad experience when you were younger and that the peach pie and ice cream triggered some sad and angry feelings in you, because they were part of the memory too. Not the bad part, but still part of it."

He stops talking and I look up at him. "And?"

42

"That's it. I think if you want her to know any more than that it's your place to tell her, not mine."

I don't know what to say. Again. Mark being all up in my business pisses me off something fierce, but I know he's right, I can't stop him from calling whoever he wants to. What I really want is for everybody just to leave me the hell alone, and I'm pretty sure that's not going to happen.

Betty wants me to talk to Nancy; Mark wants me to talk to Nancy, and, if she could talk, Frankie would tell me to pick up the damn phone.

All these people trying to tell me what to do, and I'm not going to put up with it. I start to tell Mark to go to hell, go to heaven, I don't care where you go, just get away from me, and tell Betty the same thing. I figure when I do that they'll throw me out, and I'm starting to think that's what ought to happen. Going to happen sooner or later, anyway.

So I start to tell him that, and I can't look at him, and I think, don't be a goddamn coward, Boone, you got to at least face the man. I raise my head and he's sitting there, waiting, and he doesn't look mad or disgusted or disappointed or anything. I shrug my shoulders and start to put my head back down so I don't have to see his eyes on me.

Then he picks up the tray and holds it out toward me. "You want a sandwich? It's ham, and it's good. I've already had one and I'm getting ready to have another one. Why don't we eat a bite and you can tell me all about Mr. Vandergriff. I saw you talking to him, or I guess I should say I saw you listening to him. Did he let you say anything this time?"

Chapter Six

I keep thinking about what Tiny did with the still, that camouflage job. I knew right where it was and almost didn't see it. Hell, I didn't see it, not at all. That was pretty damn smart. I'm thinking we need to get another batch going, that's for sure.

That first batch we made, last fall before the leaves fell and it got to be too risky, with people roaming all over the mountains for hunting season and all, was okay but Gamaliel's was definitely better. I need to remember to measure stuff this time and write it down somewhere. Following his directions without him there to keep an eye on things, well, it was passable. That's about the best I could say about it. I could tell by the look on Tiny's face after that first sip that he felt the same way. We even triple filtered one jug and it helped, but still, not right. Not bad enough to throw out, not good enough to brag on.

I call Tiny and say, "That dog of yours, maybe it wants to get together with Frankie now that they've both been cut on so they can talk about what assholes people are. You going to be around in the next day or so?"

"Eunuch's okay, pretty much made peace with what they did down at the shelter. If Frankie could use a sympathetic ear I guess we could accommodate them. How about day after tomorrow, about middle morning?"

"Let me check," I say, and turn to Frankie. "Hey, girl, you want to go see Eunuch and Tiny in a day or so?"

"She says sure, we'll be there," I say, and Tiny laughs. "We ought to talk about some stuff while the dogs are off feeling sorry for themselves."

"You know, I was thinking the same thing the other day. Everything's greening up real good, pretty soon you won't be able to see fifty feet through the woods."

Okay, so he knows what I want to talk about. "Good deal. See you then."

The day before I'm supposed to meet up with Tiny I get Frankie on her leash and make the rounds of the usual folks. I wait until after lunch today; the sun is out and that usually gets everybody outside for at least a little while.

Eliot Vandergriff sees me and raises up his hand. Frankie's not with anybody yet, just kind of nosing around, so we head his way. He's sitting on one of the benches next to that pitiful little fountain. I keep thinking that somebody ought to clean that pond out, try to make it look like something. Frankie's out ahead of me and gets to Mr. Vandergriff in time to nudge her head up under his hand before I catch up to her.

He laughs and says, "That's a fine dog you've got there, young man. I had one a lot like her when I was just a kid."

"Really?" I say. "What was its name?"

I've figured out that all I have to do is ask one or two questions with somebody like Vandergriff and they take over from there. Pretty soon he's telling a story about this dog that must've been smarter than any person I ever knew.

"And then there was that time he saved my life, sure did," he's saying, and Frankie pulls away from him and starts growling real low.

"What's the matter with your dog?" he says, and he's got kind of a tremble in his voice. "She's not mean, is she? I don't want anything to do with a mean dog."

"No, Mr. Vandergriff, Frankie's not mean at all," I say, looking around for whatever's got her so worked up. "She's heard something or smelled something, is all. She likes you, remember she came up to you and you were petting her? She was loving that, I could tell."

"Wel-l-l," he says, kind of like he doesn't believe me. "You sure about that?"

I'm about to answer him when Frankie moves so fast she almost jerks the leash out of my hand. She's growling louder now and straining toward the corner of the building.

Mr. Vandergriff is calling for somebody to take him back inside, and I'm trying to hold on to Frankie, but it's hard. She's pulling hard, so hard she almost chokes and has to ease up herself. I take a step toward her and the leash goes slack. She's standing there, facing the corner, hair standing up all along her back, and I get to her side just as Jerry steps around the corner.

"I knew it was you the other day, Jerry," I say, trying to keep my voice steady. What I want to do is jump him and knock his ass down. Seeing him brings back all those bad feelings about almost missing Gamaliel's service, which I'm still dead certain was because of him. I never thought Carrie would do something like that.

He's coming toward me now, real slow. One leg is pretty stiff, and he kind of swings it around when it's time to step forward on that side. I guess he did some damage in that wreck and all I can think of is that it serves him right. The way he was acting the last time I saw him, it wouldn't bother me if he was in a wheelchair. Wouldn't bother me at all.

"As far as I know you got no business here, Jerry," I say.

From behind me I hear Betty's voice. "Mr. Phillips, is that you? Can I help you with something?"

"I didn't come here to talk to you, Mrs. Franklin," he says. He's stopped again and we're standing about ten feet apart. I've got Frankie's leash wrapped around my hand and for now she's okay, but I can feel the tension in her even though we're not touching. Betty comes up and stands right beside me, her hand on mine where the leash is wrapped tight.

He goes on. "I came here to speak to Boone." He looks me right in the eye. "Is there some place we can talk?"

Chapter Seven

"You and me, we got nothing to talk about," I say. I'm staring right back at him.

It's been eight or nine months since the car wreck, so I'm guessing the leg thing is probably permanent. I only saw him once since that day, and that was at Gamaliel's service. He was as full of hate that day as I am right now, and I can't think of one single thing that he and I might have to discuss.

I wonder if Carrie's going to come around the corner next. With that leg he'd have a hard time driving.

"Mrs. Phillips isn't with me, Boone," Jerry says, like he can read my mind or something. "I didn't tell her where I was going. I thought this first meeting ought to be between the two of us."

"There is not a damn thing that you and I have to have any kind of meeting about," I say, and I'm trying real hard not to shout at him or turn Frankie loose on him. She's still behaving herself, but I can tell she would go after him in a heartbeat if I gave the word.

I turn to Betty. "I'm going on back to the house, Betty. You might want to do something about that trash in your yard." I give the leash a little pull. "C'mon, Frankie, let's go back home."

We start back toward the little house and I hear Jerry say, "I have to talk to you, Boone! It's part of my program!"

We keep walking, and I don't look back to see if he's trying to limp after us. He's talking to my back now, shouting, "I have to make amends!"

I don't have any idea what he's talking about, and if I did I wouldn't believe a thing that asshole said. "He's got a lot of damn nerve coming around here," I tell Frankie. We get to the house and go inside. I take the leash off of Frankie and she goes straight to the water dish and then to her blanket. I look down at my hands and they're trembling a little.

In a few minutes I'm settled down and about ready to head for the kitchen and mix up an S&S when there's a knock on the door. For a second I think about just ignoring it, but then there's another knock and I figure, what the hell, and open the front door.

Mark and Betty are standing there, and, before I can say anything, Mark says, "He's gone, Boone. I watched him pull out of the parking lot. After you walked off he stood there for a minute, looking at the ground, and then went right to his car."

Betty looks at Frankie and then at me. "Are you two all right?"

"Frankie, Betty wants to know if you're okay," I say, and Frankie gets up and trots right over to Betty. She smiles down at the dog and then up at me.

"She looks like she's fine," she says, and then gets a real serious look on her face. "How are you, Boone? I don't know what your history is with Mr. Phillips, besides that thing with Maryanne in my office when you were asking about how Gamaliel passed on, but today you were about as mad as I've ever seen you."

I shake my head. I really don't want to talk to Betty about Jerry. I scratch the scar on my arm, and out of the corner of my eye I see Mark nodding at me.

"Betty, if you have things to do I'll stay here for a while," he says. "I'd like to talk to Boone about some of the stories anyway."

Betty is looking at Mark and turns back to me. "Are you sure you're all right, Boone?"

"I'm fine, Betty. You should check on Mr. Vandergriff. That's where we were when Frankie, I guess she smelled him, when Frankie knew Jerry was coming and I think it might have scared Vandergriff a little."

"I'll do that right now, Boone. You're sure you're okay?"

I nod to Betty. I'm tired of saying I'm okay over and over. It's like they don't believe me.

She turns back to Mark. "I'll talk to you later, Mark."

"Okay, Betty."

She finally leaves and Mark says, "So, you have anything to drink here?"

I can't believe what he's asking and then realize he's not talking about what I thought. "I've got Thunderstorm and water, is all."

"No sweet tea? You sure you're from the South?"

I start to say something and look over and see the grin on his face. I don't like being teased, but I guess he didn't mean anything by it.

"Sorry, no sweet tea," I say and try to smile at Mark.

"All right, then, I guess I'll try a Thunderstorm," he says.

I pour a couple of glasses and we sit down next to each other on the couch.

"So, what was all that about?" he says after a sip.

"I don't know, Mark, I don't know why he came around or what he was talking about. I hated leaving Gamaliel's house, but at least it meant I didn't have to deal with that asshole any more, and now here he is."

Mark doesn't say anything for a minute or two, and I don't either. I've never liked talking just to be talking, which is one reason I liked Gamaliel so much. We could just sit and watch the world go by and it was okay with both of us. Tiny's kind of like that, too, now that I think about it. We talk pretty easy, but neither one of us feels like we have to.

"You said you didn't know what Jerry was talking about," Mark finally says. "Betty told me what he said to you right there at the end, and I'm pretty sure I do know."

So what he said to Betty about wanting to talk about the stories from the old folks was just a bullshit way to get rid of her. I didn't think preachers did that kind of thing. Maybe he's not such a better than you kind of guy after all.

"Okay, so you're thinking I care about what he was talking about. I really don't, Mark, I don't want to have anything to do with him. Nothing."

"Well, if I'm right, he might need to have something to do with you."

"You don't have any idea what he's done to me," I say, looking at the glass of Thunderstorm and thinking hard about going into the kitchen and topping it off with shine.

"No, I don't, and unless you want to tell me, I don't need to know," Mark says. "But let me ask you something. Was Jerry a drinker? or a drug user?"

I laugh out loud. "Every time he came around Gamaliel's house he was drunk on his ass," I say. "It's a thousand wonders he went as long as he did without running his car off the road."

Mark nods. "I thought so. Betty said he told you something about a program and making amends."

I shrug. "I didn't listen to what he had to say, and don't plan to listen to him if he comes back around. I told Carrie two years ago that if he'd leave me alone I'd leave him alone, and I've stood by that. But he won't go away. That piece of shit just keeps showing up, over and over again."

He doesn't say anything to that, and for a minute we just sit there on the couch, until finally I say, "Mark, if you've got something you want to say I wish you'd go ahead and say it."

He takes a deep breath and blows it out hard between his lips, and says, "I think Jerry's in a 12-step program, Boone."

"I don't know what you're talking about, Mark." I don't want to talk about Jerry with Mark or anybody else; it just makes me mad all over again.

Mark stands up and starts walking around. It's not a big room, so he only takes a few steps before he has to turn around, but he goes back and forth a few times before he says anything.

"If Jerry was a drinker, and it got so out of control that he was wrecking his life, then he might have joined AA."

I heard something once about something called AA but I don't know what it is or a 12-step program either and tell Mark so.

"It's something some people do when they figure out that they need to stop drinking, or smoking crack, or meth, or taking pills, or anything like that. There's programs for all kinds of addictions, and AA is the oldest. It's for drinkers, and from what little bit you've told me about Jerry, he might be somebody that needs that."

I don't say anything.

Mark keeps going. "Anyway, one of the parts of the program is to go to people you've wronged in some way and try to make it right. It's what they call making amends, and if he's treated you wrong in the past, I'll bet you're on his list."

I stand up so Mark and I are face to face there in front of the couch.

"Look, Mark, Jerry's a liar and a bully and he's tried to kill me at least once." I don't want to even think about Jerry trying to do anything worthwhile; every time I think about him I just get madder and madder. That's what's happening right now.

"I don't know anything about any list, and if he's got one I sure don't want to be on it, If all you want to do is talk about Jerry you probably ought to get on out of here."

Mark starts to say something and then stops. He's looking at me like he really wants to keep going, but finally he nods his head real slow and says, "Okay, Boone. Betty and I wanted to make sure you're all right. If you decide sometime you want to talk about this, let me know. I'll listen to you. These old folks aren't the only ones who need to tell their story, you know."

He leans over and pats Frankie on the head. "Keep an eye on him, girl. Okay?"

Frankie doesn't care what he's saying, as long as he's saying it to her.

He straightens up and looks over at me. "See you later, Boone. Let me know when you have more memories from the old folks."

He closes the door and I watch him walk back toward the chapel. He opens the door to the chapel and goes inside and I head for the kitchen and mix a nice strong S&S.

This is one of those times when I would really like to talk to Nancy. Wonder what she's doing right now.

I put the glass down and pick up the phone and stand there like an idiot for what has to be two minutes before I put it back down. The S&S is about half gone and I fill it back up and take it into the living room. Frankie comes over and lays her head on my leg, and I give her a scratch.

That damn Jerry. Who does he think he is, coming back around here? "I could have gone the rest of my life without laying eyes on that guy," I tell Frankie.

I try to remember how the day started, and I can't. Seeing Jerry is what this day is now, and I can't make that go away. I don't even try the TV; all that time at Gamaliel's without it, I kind of got used to not watching. I mean, I like some of the cop shows okay, but right now I'm not in the mood, and most of what's on is a bunch of crap. I'm not very smart and even I know that. Some of my friends can't go half a day without sitting down for an hour or two.

Then I think, what friends? Since I ran Nancy off, Tiny's about it. The old folks here don't count, not really. There's not a one of them anywhere close to the kind of guy Gamaliel was. Man, I miss him. It didn't matter that he was old as dirt. He was a friend of mine, and thinking about him being gone for good starts the tears up again, even though it's been months.

Chapter Eight

Three or four days later I'm back at the fountain, talking to Eliot Vandergriff's son Raymond. He's good about coming around to check on his old man, a lot better than most of the families here. He's some big businessman, drives a convertible with two seats and a really long hood, and it sounds like it would tear up the road. I've never driven anything but Daddy's piece of shit truck. Actually, I guess it's mine now; I put the title in the safety deposit box with Gamaliel's money, which I guess is my money now, too. It's hard for me to think about that, about it being my money and all. I started out keeping it for Gamaliel and I guess I still kind of think I'm doing that.

Raymond says, "Your dog gave Daddy quite a scare a while back."

"I figured that," I say. "Is he still worked up about it, or can I bring Frankie back around when he's out here?"

He doesn't answer right away. Instead, he says, "Mind telling me what that was all about? Daddy never was very clear, just told me that the dog scared him out of a year's life. I don't believe in that kind of thing, but Daddy does." He looks over at me like I'm supposed to apologize or something.

I start to tell him that if his daddy's such a baby that he can't be around a dog that wasn't even going after him, maybe I shouldn't be spending any time with him. What I say instead is, "I'd just as soon not."

He looks down at Frankie, and she looks back with that kind of a grin she's got.

"Well," he says, "Maybe I'll talk to Mrs. Franklin then. Can't have an animal around Daddy that gets out of control." He stands up and dusts off his rear end, then he straightens his tie and hitches up his pants, looking down at me the whole time. I look over at Frankie, and she's still grinning.

"Well," I say, "You do what you feel like you have to."

He starts toward the main building and I look back at Frankie. "Did you see him dusting off that fat ass of his, Frankie?" I say, real low.

Out of the corner of my eye I see him stop for just a second, then he starts walking faster.

I try to stay away from Mr. Vandergriff for the next few days. It's pretty easy because he doesn't call me over like he used to and also because I look for anybody else to talk to besides him. That's how I end up talking to Mr. Stannard, Melvin Stannard. He's only been here a week or so and mostly he sits in one of the gliders with a pile of books beside him and reads. I can tell he's serious about this reading stuff because sometimes his lips are moving, and sometimes he'll stop and close the book with his finger inside to hold his place and stare off toward the mountains. A couple of times he laughed out loud, and once when I was walking pretty close behind him I saw him shake his head and heard him say, "Damn!" kind of whispery. I never got all worked up about a book in my life, and he was like that almost every time I saw him.

Frankie takes to him right off, and he's had dogs before, I can tell that by the way he acts around her. He's awful unsteady on his feet, but I swear if he wasn't he and Frankie'd be running all over the place. Pretty soon Frankie is dragging me over to Mr. Stannard whenever she sees him in the yard.

The next time I see Mark I start to tell him about Mr. Stannard, how I don't have any stories yet but that he's real good with Frankie, but he stops me and says, "We have a couple of things to talk about, Boone. Let's go into my office."

I've never had it be a good thing when somebody tells me to go to the office, any kind of office, so I

61

figure that Mr. Vandergriff's son has been making trouble for me and Frankie.

"Close the door, Boone," Mark says, and he has this serious tone in his voice, and I'm thinking, oh, shit.

I close the door and stand there, not sure what to do next. What I want to do is open the door and take Frankie back down to my house, but I'm thinking that Mark would just follow me down there. So I stand there like a damn idiot until Mark says, "Why don't you have a seat?"

I start toward the chair he's pointing at and I'm ready to sit down when there's a knock on the door I just closed. Mark says, "Come in," and the door swings open.

First Betty comes in, and then a woman and a little girl, about nine or ten, looks like. It takes me a second to realize that it's Aunt Claire and Hannah.

It's not that Hannah looks all that different, but it's been over a year since I saw her last. She's had one of those growth spurts and has to be half a foot taller than she was when I put her on the school bus. Aunt Claire I've mostly seen in pictures, but she hasn't changed all that much. A little fatter, I guess, and her hair looks awful. I reckon it's supposed to be blonde but it looks yellow to me, like those flowers Momma used to put out in the side yard, I can't remember what she called them. Anyway, I know it's Claire.

Hannah runs over to the chair and I stand up and she throws her arms around me and hangs on so tight I can hardly breathe, and I can feel myself starting to cry. I don't want to do that, not in front of all these people especially, so I kind of push her away and say, "Hannah, this is my dog. I didn't have her when you left." Then I think, that's stupid, of course she knows that I didn't have a dog when she left.

Hannah looks down at her and then up at me. "She's pretty. What's her name?"

"Frankie."

Her eyes get real big and she drops down on her knees in front of Frankie and nobody in the room is saying anything, anything at all. She and Frankie are looking at each other and then Frankie does that thing she used to do with Gamaliel where she scoots in real close. Hannah reaches up and scratches her behind one ear and finally whispers, "Hi, Frankie."

I look around and I'm not the only one that's about to cry; even Mark's eyes are wet, but he's got a big smile on his face, watching Hannah and Frankie.

Claire clears her throat and Mark looks at her and frowns and shakes his head a little. She shrugs her shoulders and doesn't say anything, and the only noise in the room is Hannah, talking to Frankie so

63

soft that I can't make out any words, but Frankie is eating this up, all this attention.

After a minute Hannah stands up and says, "She's great, Boone, I just love her."

Then Mark says, "Let me bring in another chair or two so we can sit and talk." He's out the door and back before I can ask him what we have to talk about.

"Claire, are you ready to tell us why you wanted everybody here?"

Mark is talking real nice and soft, but he's making sure everybody knows this is his office. He's looking around, not staring at anybody, but in a few seconds he's got everybody looking at him. He stops looking around and his eyes settle on Aunt Claire. She's sitting up straight as a fence post, looking back at Mark.

I'm watching Hannah.

I'm trying to think of the last time I saw her, I guess it was when I took her to the bus that morning after Momma took off and before Daddy did what he did. I hadn't thought about it much, but I think it's a good thing that Momma got her out of there before that happened. If I'd had to deal with Daddy and Hannah I don't know what I would have done.

Since I made that phone call after I moved out of Gamaliel's house, Hannah and I have talked on the phone two or three times, and she kept saying I needed to get up there, but I hadn't yet, and now here she is. She's got her daddy's face, and that's too bad. Every time I look at her I see Daddy.

She turns and catches me looking at her and smiles a little, but it's a sad smile, and then she looks back at Mark. We're all looking at him now, me included, and I'm sitting there with my hand on Frankie's neck thinking, so now what?

"Claire?" says Mark, and she breaks off looking at him and drops her head, looking at the floor now.

Nobody says anything for what seems like a long time, and then Claire says, "I heard from Natalie."

Hannah says, "Really? What did Momma say? Is she coming back to live here? When did you talk to her?" and on and on, a thousand miles an hour. I don't say anything, because I don't know how I feel about Momma any more. The last time I saw her she was in Jake's car, driving away without saying a damn thing to me, while Jake was stealing my truck.

"Why did you come all the way down here to tell us that?" I say.

Mark frowns at me and shakes his head a little. I know I'm supposed to keep my mouth shut, but the only way I can do that is leave. I'm about to get up when Claire says, "She wants to see her children. She's out in Memphis all by herself, and she's lonely and scared. She wants to see you and Hannah, Boone."

"Well, she can tell Jake to drive her back." I've never even been to Knoxville and don't have any idea where Memphis is, except I'm pretty sure it's west of here. Or south, maybe.

"Jake's gone," Claire says. "Sounds like they had a big fight, and he took off, and she's out there by herself. He took the car, that lousy son of — "

"Claire!" Mark says.

She looks at him and her face gets a little red.

I look down at Frankie and then over at Hannah. She's sitting there with her hands in her lap, twisting them around like she's wringing out a dishcloth.

"So," Claire starts talking again, "you see, Boone, how that's not going to happen."

"So what do you want from me?"

"I was thinking you could go get her and bring her back home. She needs family around her, Boone."

I start laughing out loud, and she opens her mouth but before she can say anything I say, "You mean in that piece of shit truck that Daddy left me?"

Mark starts to say something and I wave my hand at him. "There is no way I could drive that thing to the next county, much less to Memphis, wherever that is."

Mark holds up his hand. "What I was trying to say, Boone, is that I agree with you. Not your language, you know that, but about the truck making it to Memphis. It's almost 400 miles each way. I'm on the internet now and it looks like a bus ticket would cost about $50. Claire, can you get an address from Natalie where we could send a money order for, let's say, $100 to get a ticket and whatever else she needs until she gets back here?"

Claire nods, and Hannah lights up with this big smile. I don't say anything, because I'm still not sure I want to see her again.

"Momma's coming home? Where's she going to stay? Can she stay with us, Aunt Claire?" Hannah is lit up like a Christmas tree.

"Only thing is," says Claire, and I think, here it comes. Always something.

"Only thing is, I don't think it's a good idea for her to ride all that way by herself. There's bad people on those buses. I still think you should go get her, Boone."

"What about you? Why can't you go get her?"

Claire is shaking her head before I even finish talking. "I can't, Boone, I have responsibilities, and, besides, I have to take care of Hannah. Right, baby doll?"

Hannah looks like she doesn't know what to say. Finally she says, "I'm big enough to stay by myself, Aunt Claire. I'd be fine, I promise."

"No, honey, it's not like it was before your uncle went to be with the Lord. I couldn't leave you in that big old house for that long."

Everybody turns and looks at me.

I know what they're thinking. They think I need to go to Memphis and get Momma, and if I don't then I'm some kind of lousy son.

They don't know what it was like before she left. Well, maybe Hannah knows, but nobody else. How I always felt like I had to keep Daddy from hurting her, and how when I couldn't stop him she'd just take it, never fight back, and then as soon as she got away from Daddy she took up with this Jake guy who isn't much better, looks like. I like it the way it is right now, me and Frankie and Tiny. It'd be damn near perfect if Nancy was around, and I know I need to fix that giant screwup that was all my fault, every bit of it.

Anyway, things are pretty good right now. Hell, they're better than pretty good. I get along just fine without Momma around. She left me to deal with Daddy, and then helped Jake try to steal my truck. I've already made my peace with her being out there somewhere with whoever, and it sounds like these people want to stir all that shit up again. Well, they can do it without my help. I need to talk to Mark about this, and about Nancy. I turn to Mark, my hand still on Frankie's head. She's being awfully good, sitting through this without making a sound.

"Mark, I need to talk to you after this meeting thing is over, okay?"

68

Chapter Nine

Mark finally gets everybody out of his office by telling them he's going to talk to me privately. They all think he's going to try to talk me into going to Memphis on a bus to get Momma and bring her back here. I'm pretty sure Betty is on Claire's side in this thing, even though she didn't say anything, and Hannah just wants Momma back here. I don't really care what they think, I'm not going to do it.

Part of it is that the only bus I've ever been on is the school bus back when I was little, and I hated every minute of it. Everybody could see what a dump I lived in, since our little road was the turnaround for it to head back toward town. I knew they were laughing at my house and my clothes and there were always three or four people giving me shit the whole way to the school. So I don't like buses, and if Memphis is that far away, it'd be a long ride.

And there's leaving all my stuff in the house for however long I'd be gone and hoping nobody went snooping around.

Mostly, though, I can't see leaving Frankie for that long.

When it's down to me and Mark he doesn't sit down. Instead he looks at me and says, "Want to get out of this room for a while?"

I look down at Frankie and I'm about to ask her what she thinks and Mark says, "She'll be okay in your house for a little while, won't she?"

He comes over to me and puts his car keys in my hand. "Let's go for a drive."

"Listen, Mark," I say. "I've never driven anything besides the truck. I'm not sure — "

"I'm not sending you off by yourself, Boone. I'm coming along for the ride. You can drive for a while and then I'll take over. Okay?"

I don't know what to say, so I don't say anything.

"After you get Frankie settled in, come on out to the parking lot. You know which car's mine?"

I shake my head. I never paid attention to who drove what, except for Mr. Vandergriff's son. He has that fancy sports car.

"It'll be the one I'm standing beside."

He's got a little grin on his face and I can't help but smile back at him. "Be out there in a minute."

Frankie's not used to me going off and leaving her in the house, but I give her a handful of food and say, "Just for a few minutes, girl, and I'll be back." She's busy eating when I go out the door, and she looks up for a second when I have to come back in and get the key to lock the door.

It's not a big lot, but it takes me a second to find Mark. He's standing beside this little boxy thing, looks like I could pick it up and set it up in the grass.

"Got the keys?" he asks.

I nod.

"Okay, then, unlock it and let's get going. If we stand here long enough somebody's going to come looking for me."

There's only one key on the ring, so I get it unlocked without any trouble. Mark gets in the passenger side and I slide behind the wheel.

"Damn," I say, in a kind of whisper, and I hear Mark laugh. Any other time I'd have got mad about being laughed at, but this seat is so comfortable I just let it go.

"Okay," he says, "It's a five speed. You know how to drive a five speed?"

I shake my head. "Truck's an automatic."

He sighs. "Okay, maybe I'll drive this time. We need to get you out on the road in this car, though. Loads of fun to drive."

"Looks like a good wind'd blow it right off the road."

Mark grins. "Let's switch places."

He drives like a bat out of hell, and I'm holding on around every curve. As far as I can tell, he's not using the brake at all. I look over at Mark and he's got this huge smile on his face, he's like I've never seen him before.

We end up in a part of the county I've never seen before, and he pulls into a gravel parking lot and stops. There's a stand of cedar trees in front of us and half a dozen picnic tables. Through the trees I can see water.

When we get out and walk through the woods, it's almost like being up at the pool above the house next to Gamaliel's. Except the woods are all cleaned out, and there's a trail and these tables and when we get to the water there's a deck that sticks out into the lake. Two guys are sitting at one end and I can't tell whether they are asleep or fishing. Mark heads to the other side of the deck and we sit with our legs over the side and for a few minutes don't say anything. I can hear the water slapping against the rocks and every once in a while a bird flies down low, almost touching the water. It's as nice a place as I've been in a long, long time.

I can feel Mark's eyes on me and pretty soon he says, "So what did you want to talk about?"

"I sure wish Nancy was here," I say, and then look at Mark. "No offense."

"None taken," he says. "You know, I talked to her the other day."

And all of a sudden I'm scared. I'm afraid to find out what they said to each other. I figure it's got to be bad, or he would have come and told me as soon as it happened. I sit there with my head down staring at the water and eventually say, "What did you two talk about?"

He puts his hand on my shoulder and I jerk away. I don't like people touching me. He lets his hand drop and doesn't try that again.

"Mostly we talked about you, Boone."

"Do I want to hear this, Mark?"

He takes his time about answering.

"She called me because she didn't know what went wrong the last time she saw you, and it scared her," he says.

"What did you tell her?"

"I told her that you were holding on to a bad memory from when you were young and that you weren't mad at her."

"What else?"

"Nothing else. She asked and I said that she should talk to you."

My Daddy told me over and over again that you couldn't trust preachers, and that a nigger would just

73

as soon stab you in the back as look at you. One more thing he was wrong about, I guess. Now that I think about it, he's the only person I ever heard use that word. Nobody else.

I can't look him in the eye. I hate owing people anything; seems like they always held it over me for way too long. But I know I owe Mark, and there's nothing I can do about it now.

"So, do you think I ought to call her?"

"Well, I sort of told her to expect a call from you, so, yes, I think you should."

I can see him move out of the corner of my eye; he's getting up. Then he hands me his cell phone. "I'm going for a walk. Be back in about ten minutes."

When he gets back I hand him the phone.

"What did she say?"

"I didn't talk to her, had to leave her a message." I hate doing that, talking to a machine.

He nods. "Good enough. Ready to head back?"

On the way back he takes it slower and we talk about Momma.

"Don't you want to see her again?"

"I don't know, Mark, I just don't know. Mostly no, I guess. I mean, you know she left me there, didn't even say goodbye, and then helped Jake try to steal the truck." I think about forgiving her, but it makes me mad every time I think about the way she dumped me and then Hannah.

74

"Forgiveness is a powerful thing, Boone." It's like he is listening to what I'm thinking. He goes on, "And I think you may get some more practice with Jerry sometime soon."

Now why did he have to bring up that asshole? I go from being worried about Nancy to mad in about a half a second. Nobody, not Mark or anybody else, tells me who I need to forgive. I'm mad at Momma, but I wouldn't turn away from her if I saw her on the street. Jerry, I might just take a swing at him on general principles. I don't even know why Mark is talking about Jerry. It's none of his damn business, and I start to tell him so.

He lets go of the wheel with his right hand and holds it up. "Before you say anything, Boone, think about this. You're asking Nancy to do some forgiving, and I know it's not the same thing, not at all, but maybe the forgiveness part is."

I don't buy that for a minute.

I mean, what I did to her was nothing like what Momma did to me and Hannah, and Jerry, well, I know it'll be a cold day in hell before I even think about forgiving him. The bastard pulled a knife on me. And he tried to keep me from saying goodbye to Gamaliel. That's too much to forgive.

The next few days I end up spending a lot of time with Melvin. He tells me to stop calling him Mr. Stannard, and that makes me think of Gamaliel. He's like Gamaliel in a bunch of ways; real different, too, like I never saw Gamaliel crack a book the whole time I knew him, and Melvin's always got two or three he's carrying around. Today I ask him about what he's reading. It's a little book, not like most of what I see him with, and he says, "It's called 'A Separate Peace'. You might like it, Boone. It's about two young men and, well, I won't tell you how the story goes. It's very good. I read it again every few years. You should give it a try."

I'm probably not going to do that. When I was in school I barely read what they said I had to, and I'm out now. I'm sure not going to do any more reading.

Aside from the reading stuff, though, he reminds me a lot of the old man. Melvin wants to do for himself and doesn't take any shit from anybody, he's got great stories, and Frankie thinks he's okay. I'm glad he moved in here. I have to be careful to see some of the other old folks, the ones I had started getting to know.

Mark keeps saying he's going to get me out on the road behind the wheel of his little car, he calls it his Mini, but so far he hasn't. We are getting a good amount of stories now, and he and Betty seem to be real happy with how that's working. Betty still hasn't said anything about Mr. Vandergriff's son complaining to her about Frankie, and I'm sure not going to bring it up.

I'm pretty torn up about whether or not to keep calling Nancy. She never got back to me when I called her on Mark's phone, and I go back and forth between getting Frankie and driving over there and just giving up. The giving up idea makes me sad and angry, though, and the going over there scares the hell out of me. So I don't know what to do.

Then I step out of the house with Frankie, getting ready to do our rounds, and she's walking toward me, almost at the front door. Frankie starts going crazy, of course, and she's looking at him and smiling and then she looks up at me and her face changes and it's like she's careful. Like she's afraid I'm going to yell at her or something.

I've seen that look before, but it was on Momma, and she was looking at Daddy.

Chapter Ten

I try to think of something to say and all I can think of is, "Hey, Nancy."

She's back to looking at Frankie and Frankie's out at the end of her leash, only a foot or two from Nancy. I take a long step toward her and she squats down and puts her arms around my dog and starts whispering in her ear.

I'm watching the two of them and thinking how mad I am at Daddy for still being inside my head. All this meanness, not trusting anybody, this being mad all the time, I feel like he's in there just egging me on.

I finally get up the nerve to say, "You want to come in for a minute?"

She looks at me and then at Frankie. "What do you say, girl? You want some company?"

She stands up and brushes her hands on her jeans. "Sure. Let's go on in."

I try to open the door for her and get all tangled up in the leash, and she laughs, and I'll be damned if

I don't feel that flash of anger, somebody laughing at me. I keep my head down so she can't see my face and work on the leash, and I'm telling myself to stop being stupid. I've been missing her like crazy and here she is, and I'm already mad at her.

It seems like it takes me a long time to get untangled, but by the time I do I'm over being mad and I open the door and she and Frankie go in ahead of me. I unsnap Frankie's leash and she goes right to Nancy and looks up at her like this is all she needs in the world.

Nancy's got her hand on Frankie's head and looks around and for a minute neither one of us says anything. Then I say, "You want to sit down?" and I think, damn, it used to be easy to talk to her and now I'm afraid to say anything.

She nods and goes over to the couch.

She sits on the end and it's like she makes sure Frankie is between us if I sit on the couch, too, and I stand there like a fool for a second and then sit down on the other end.

We're quiet again and then we both start to say something at the same time and stop and I look up at her and say, "Go ahead."

"No, you go ahead."

I shake my head. Then I look at Frankie and laugh a little and say, "Maybe Frankie should go first."

She nods and says, "That's a good idea. Frankie, what do you say? You want to start things off?"

Frankie wiggles around like she can't stand to feel this good, and Nancy laughs and so do I and I think, good girl, Frankie.

Nancy's petting Frankie and I take a deep breath and say, "Mark said he talked to you."

She nods and says, "He didn't tell me much, said I should ask you."

There's another of those silences and I finally break it.

"Tiny tells me I'm a fool."

She gives me a look. "You're not a fool, Boone. I wish you'd tell me what's going on, but if Tiny told you I said that, I might have to beat him up the next time I see him."

That almost makes me smile.

"You want to know about the pie, right?"

I'm staring at the floor and when I look up she's shaking her head, hard.

"I want to know why you're right on the edge of being mad so much of the time. It scares me, Boone, I can't help it."

"Can we start with the pie?" I don't think I even know why I get mad so easy, besides kind of always being mad at Daddy for being such a son of a bitch, but I know she's right, and I don't want to scare her.

She doesn't answer me, just sits there with her hand on Frankie's head, scratching behind her left ear.

"Thing is, some of this stuff I've never told anybody," I say, and it feels like I'm getting too close to something, and if I keep going I won't be able to stop.

Nancy doesn't say a word, and she's stopped scratching Frankie's ear.

"So when I was little Momma used to make a pie for whoever died, I mean for their family, you know," and I tell her all about the time she made one just for us and we were having a piece right out of the oven with some ice cream and Daddy came home all drunk and mad and threw it in the yard, and I'm about to tell her a lot more and barely stop myself and end up saying, "I'm real sorry I was such an asshole when you came around, Nancy, what you tried to do was awful nice and I ruined it for both of us."

She doesn't say anything and I say, "Truth is, I've been scared to call you," and then I manage to shut myself up.

"Truth is," she says, "if you'd called right after that happened, I'd've probably hung up on you."

I nod. "I figured that."

Frankie is almost in her lap, and I point to her and say, "Frankie sure is glad to see you." I make myself look right at her. "I am too."

Nancy doesn't answer me and after a minute I say, "I was just getting ready to take Frankie out to see the old folks. You want to come along? There's this new guy, Melvin, and he kind of reminds me of Gamaliel . . . ."

I just stop talking then and wait for her to say something, and when she doesn't, I don't know what to do.

Nancy takes a deep breath, lets it out, and stands up. "Listen, Boone, I have to get out of here. I promised Mom I'd help with dinner tonight, and I haven't even been to the store yet."

She bends down to Frankie and gives her a final pat and, when she stands up, turns to me and says, "I'm glad you told me what happened with your folks. It sort of makes sense, what you did, now that I know that. But you've got to tell me this stuff, Boone, you can't keep it hid. Otherwise I'll be tiptoeing around you all the time, and I can't do that, you know?"

I nod and say, "I know."

She says, "I'll call you sometime soon, maybe we can do something together."

"I'd like that a lot," I say, and I'm thinking maybe I haven't screwed this up after all.

Chapter Eleven

It's another three or four days before she calls me, and I spend a lot of it with Melvin. He's a pretty funny guy, and a lot smarter than I am. He's not a jerk about it, though, so I don't mind so much having to ask him to explain stuff over and over again.

I find out that his wife died in 1998, when they were living in Brazil. I don't know anything about Brazil, not even where it is, but when I ask Melvin about it he ignores me. He'll talk your ear off about almost anything you can think of, so I guess it must hurt to think about Brazil. He won't even tell me how much longer he stayed there after his wife died. I know before he came to the home he lived in a bunch of places, and he can tell stories about Texas, and Ohio, and some place called Prince Edward Island. He's been all over.

"So how come you lived so many places?" I ask him. The main reason we moved from one place to another when I was a kid was because Daddy owed somebody money or did something to piss off the guy that owned whatever house we were living in.

"Never had the same job for more than four years," he says, and winks at me. "Always somewhere new to go, Boone. You should try it, you know. You're young, healthy, you should just get in the truck and go."

"Have you seen my truck, Melvin?"

He laughs. "Okay, maybe not that exact vehicle. Still, you should go."

"Hell, Melvin, I've never even been to Knoxville."

"Then you should begin there."

When I tell Mark about this, he doesn't laugh, which is what I figured he was going to do. Instead, he says, "I think Mr. Stannard makes a good point. Maybe you should go down to Knoxville, just to see what it's like."

The thought of going to a place like Knoxville scares me to death. Tiny's been, and he tells me about the buildings all jammed up against each other and the interstate highway with cars going eighty miles an hour, and about Market Square on a weekend night, where sometimes you can't walk from one end to the other there's so many people. There's nothing like that around here.

I tell Melvin I'll think about it, but I'm pretty sure I won't be going to Knoxville or any other place, at least not in that truck. It's good for a trip to the grocery store and up to see Tiny and that's about it.

When Nancy calls I tell her about the Knoxville thing and she says, "That's a great idea! I was going down next week to Market Square to see H.P. and the Owlettes. You should come along. Cyrus was going with me but I don't think he'd mind a bit if you went instead. He doesn't like blues music, so he could stay home, which he probably wants to do anyway, and you could come with me instead."

"When are you going?" I sure didn't expect this, and I don't know whether I like blues music or not. We didn't have much music in our house when I was growing up. Seems like Momma used to play the radio some, but only when Daddy wasn't around and only that gospel station. She knew what he'd do if he came in the house and there was a preacher on the radio. Some of those people could sing, though. I remember that. But one time I heard one of those preachers call blues the Devil's music, so I guess it won't be the same.

First time I ever set foot in Gamaliel's house he was singing that Closer Walk with Thee song and playing on the fiddle, and that was really sad. I was going to try to learn to play that thing until Jerry smashed it.

Thinking about that gets me mad all over again, and I miss what Nancy says and have to ask her to repeat it all, about the day and time and all that stuff.

"It's Thursday, that's day after tomorrow, and it starts about seven or so. They let dogs on the Square, but I don't know how Frankie would like the crowds, She'd be okay at home for a few hours, though, wouldn't she?"

"I guess so."

"Great! I'll come get you about six or so. I'll drive, since I've been down there before, and we can get a burrito before the music starts. Maybe I should come at 5:30. Okay?"

I say okay and she's gone and I hang up and think, what the hell have I gotten myself into? I've never been to Knoxville, don't know what blues music is, and never tasted a burrito. I know what one is, they advertise them on TV, and they have frozen ones in the store, but I never bought one.

This whole thing is a lot for me to think about, and it's scary for a lot of reasons. I wonder if Mark is in his office; he's pretty good to talk to most of the time.

"Frankie, you want to go see Mark?"

Frankie wants to go see anybody, anytime, so I get the leash and we head up to the main building. We go in the side door, close to Mark's office, and it's standing a little open. I knock on the door and Mark says, "Just a minute."

About a half a minute later he comes to the door and says, "Boone, sorry to keep you waiting, had to finish up a couple of letters. Come on in."

When I tell him about talking to Melvin and then Nancy calling and about the trip to Knoxville, he says, "That is a wonderful idea, Boone. If Nancy drives, you don't have to worry about traffic, and it sounds like a fun evening."

"I heard one preacher say a while back that the blues was the Devil's music."

Mark laughs. "Well, I guess it might be, if you got the Devil in you already. You don't know what the blues are?"

I shake my head.

"Man, you are in for a treat."

Thursday afternoon comes and I get dressed. I don't worry so much anymore about what I wear since I really don't go anywhere, but I did take some of the money Betty pays me and bought a couple of shirts and a pair of jeans at the Amvets store that looked like nobody had ever had them on.

I'm glad I did that, because when Nancy gets here a little before 5:30, she's in a dress and looks really good. It's not real tight or short or anything like that, but she's still really nice to look at.

She comes up to me and stands there and I finally figure out she's waiting for me to say something about how she looks, so I do.

"Damn, you look good."

She ducks her head a little and then twirls around and says, "Thanks, Boone. You look good too."

I know better than this, but I guess she felt like she ought to say something back to me. We stand looking at each other for a second and it starts to feel a little weird so I say, "Well, you want to come in for a minute? We got time for that?"

"Sure, that'd be great. You still remember how I like my S&S's?"

I'd already had one before she got here and didn't know whether to offer her one or not.

"I think so. About three drops of shine, right?"

She laughs. "I think about six, if you don't mind. I wish we were old enough to get a beer or something down on the Square."

I make one for her and another one for myself and we sit on the couch and sip and Frankie tries to climb up in Nancy's lap.

"Sorry, girl, not tonight. I'm all dressed up, can't you see?"

I sit there and sip and watch the two of them and think, Tiny and Betty and Mark are right, I'd be a damned fool to do anything to screw this up.

And then I start thinking about how she was right there with me when Gamaliel died and I'm almost getting teary-eyed. Nancy looks over at me and says, "You all right, Boone?" and I nod and reach out to pat her hand and Frankie noses me away. She starts laughing and I can't help but laugh, too, and she finishes her S&S, which is almost all Thunderstorm, and says, "Why don't we get on down toward Knoxville? Sometimes it's hard to find a place to park when there's music on the Square."

On the way down, we talk about what she's doing this summer and I don't ask about what's going to happen in the fall. She says she's not been doing much, and talks some about this group we're going to see, and outside the car are more and more cars and fewer and fewer trucks and a couple of big ones that rock the car a little, and I'm getting kind of scared. I look over at Nancy and it's like it doesn't bother her at all.

"I'm going to drive down Neyland Drive so you can see the college I'm going to."

It takes me a second to think of what to say. "You're going to college in Knoxville?", which is a pretty lame thing to say, but I say it before I think how stupid it sounds.

"Yeah," she says. "You have to get used to the drive so you can come see me."

I nod and then realize she's not looking at me, she's watching the road, and say, "I will. I mean, I'll definitely start getting used to it."

And I think, dammit, Boone, can't you open your mouth without saying something stupid?

I don't think Nancy notices how much of an idiot I've turned into, and drives along a river pointing at things and then turns up into town and it's just like Tiny said. Everything's all jammed together, there's people all over the place, and the cars are almost touching each other while they're moving down the street.

We go into this building that's nothing but cars parked one beside the other and drive around and around and finally she parks and says, "Okay, let's go get something to eat."

It's not like on TV, that's for sure. I mean, I knew what a parking garage was, seen them plenty of times, but being in one is different. Loud, and echoy, and lots of cars moving up and down. I'm glad I didn't bring Frankie, and I'm wondering what this Market Square is going to be like.

We have to stand in line to wait for a table at the place she wants to eat, and I think I'm going to crack my neck from swiveling it around. This restaurant has huge TVs all over the walls, and a long bar with maybe fifty bottles of booze on shelves behind it, and outside the people never stop walking by. It's about to wear me out just trying to keep up with it all. I look over at Nancy and she's acting like it's no big deal.

She catches me looking at her and grins. "You should see this place when somebody really popular is playing."

90

She waves her hand out at the Square, and I think, damn. If it's worse than this I don't think I want to be anywhere near it.

We get our food and there are people right behind me, so close I can barely get into my chair. I have to admit, though, the food is really good. They bring it out with big mittens on their hands and tell us not to touch the plates, and I start to ask for a Thunderstorm and Nancy says the sweet tea is good here, so that's what I have. Both of us eat every bit of food and when I get my money out Nancy says, "I asked you, remember? This is my treat."

Part of me thinks I ought to argue about that, but I don't know how this kind of stuff works, so I decide to let it go. Next time we go out I'll be sure and do the asking so I can pay. Even things out.

Maybe I'll pick a quieter place than this. Trouble is, I don't know any place to take Nancy.

I'll ask Tiny. He'll be glad to know I'm trying to make things right with her.

We finish and go out into the open air and you can still walk around but it's starting to get crowded, and then some guy shouts into a microphone, "Are you ready for some music?" and I almost jump out of my skin it's so loud and the crowd goes crazy, and then the music starts up, even louder than the guy, and everybody's jumping around and waving their hands in the air, and I'm thinking, what the hell kind of place is this?

I've never been anywhere like this before.

Chapter Twelve

It turns out I like blues music, a lot, which is good, because so does Nancy. This guy H. P. is not much older than I am, and kind of fat. Not like some people back home, some of them can't hardly get around, but this guy, all that extra weight doesn't stop him from jumping all over the stage and shouting at the crowd and screaming into the microphone and singing his ass off. The Owlettes, there are three of them, all look older than H. P. and they stand with their lips almost touching their microphones and they are right there with him. There might have been some of that gospel Momma used to listen to in there somewhere, but some of the stuff they're singing about sure isn't church stuff.

By the end of it all I'm jumping up and down with the rest of them and when it's over Nancy and I fall together and kind of hold each other up while the crowd starts to thin out.

"What did I tell you?" she's still shouting, even though she doesn't have to anymore.

"It was great!" I say, and realize I'm shouting too, and we're still holding on to each other and all of a sudden we're kissing and somebody shouts at us to get a room, whatever that means, and then I figure out what it means. It sounds like a really good idea, but I'm guessing it's not going to happen. At least not tonight.

Nancy pushes away from me and says, "So, what do you think of Knoxville so far?"

I can't answer; I'm too busy grinning.

We head back to the car and wind our way out onto the road and we're out of the city and on our way home when I say, "So how did you know about this music thing tonight?"

It's the only thing I can think of to say, but it works okay, and she tells me about all the stuff that happens in the summer down there and some of it sounds like a waste of a drive, but she's excited about all of it, so I try to pay attention. Before I know it we're back at the old folk's home and she pulls into a parking space and turns off the car.

I say, "Nancy, that was a lot better than I thought it was going to be. Cyrus doesn't know what he missed."

She laughs and says, "He doesn't care what he missed, he was so glad not to have to go spend time with his big sister."

We sit there in the quiet car for a while and then she says, "Walk you to your door?" and giggles.

On the way around the main building we don't say anything. It's so quiet here compared to where we were earlier, quiet and dark and familiar. The light's still on in my little house and we get to the front door and stop.

"You want to come in for a minute?" I say, and turn and step close to her and then we're pressed up tight against each other and it's not like that kiss down on the Square, it's just the two of us here and we're both holding on as tight as we can.

We lean back in each other's arms and she says, "If I go inside I'm thinking I won't ever come out again," and leans back in and kisses me hard and then steps back out of reach.

"Sounds good to me," I say, because I never can think of the right thing, like the stuff they say on TV that's smooth and perfect and everybody knows it.

She shakes her head. "I can't, Boone, not yet anyway. I have to go on home now. Tell Frankie hi for me, okay?" and I reach out and just miss catching her hand. She's off the porch and headed back to her car.

"I'll call you tomorrow, darlin'," I say, and I'm not sure it's loud enough for her to hear but she slows down a step and then starts back up again a little faster.

I can hear Frankie on the other side of the door getting more and more impatient, so I open the door and go on in. Just before I close it I look back up the hill and she's stopped about halfway to the parking lot and is turned around, looking back down at me, and for a second I think she's coming back but she turns again and keeps going.

Frankie acts like I've been gone a month, but did not wreck the house, so that worked out okay. I sit down with an S&S and tell her all about Market Square and the music and she listens to every word like it's real important stuff.

"And best thing was how great it was to be with Nancy," I say, and Frankie starts looking around for her and that makes me laugh.

I haven't felt this good in weeks.

The next day, when I tell Mark about my trip to Knoxville, he looks at me from across his desk and says, "I was afraid you were going to let that fine girl get away from you. Thank the Lord you came to your senses."

I still don't like all that God talk, but I know he's not going to stop, and I guess I did sort of come to my senses, when you think about it.

Melvin has a different reaction.

"You don't know about blues music? Shame on you, Boone. You've got a lot of catching up to do."

He starts rattling off names: Muddy Waters, John Lee Hooker, B. B. King, Otis Redding, Aretha Franklin, Etta James, and a lot more I'll forget as soon as I walk away from him. He says, "I've got a book in my room about the blues and how important it is to the history of American music, and you definitely need to read it. And you need to go to Memphis. You can't live in Tennessee and not go to Beale Street at least once in your life. It would be like not going to Graceland."

I'm starting to get mad at Melvin, which I have never done before. He's going on about Graceland, whatever that is, and Beale Street, and all I can think is that Memphis is where Momma is, and now seems like everybody's trying to get me to go there. My truck would never make it a thousand miles or however far it is, Jake would probably show back up and try to steal it all over again if it did make it, I've never even driven to Knoxville before, and I'm sure as hell not taking a bus there.

"No way I'm going all the way to Memphis, Melvin," I say, a little loud, I guess, because he looks at me kind of funny and says, "Okay, okay, Boone, at least let me lend you the book. I don't have it with me right now, but I'll bring it out tomorrow — "

97

"Listen, I got to go. C'mon, Frankie," and I start to take off and just leave him sitting there.

He says, "Wait, Boone, I didn't even get to tell you about my son-in-law."

I'm already standing up and so is Frankie, but I turn around and say, "What son-in-law?"

"He lives in Montreal, and he'll be here next week. I told him about you and Frankie, and how much better it is staying here with you two around to talk with, and he wants to meet you. Next Thursday, he'll be here next Thursday."

I'm about half listening, thinking about Memphis, and Aunt Claire, and Momma and Jake, and how much better it was when she was off with him and leaving us alone. And I'm wondering if I'll be able to lie to her about Daddy if she does come back around.

Actually, it wouldn't surprise me at all if Aunt Claire got a call tomorrow from Momma saying either that Jake was back or that she'd found some other guy to run around with. She sure didn't waste any time after leaving Daddy before hooking up with Jake.

"Okay, Melvin, I'll be sure and say hi to your son. Where'd you say he was from?"

"Montreal. It's in Canada."

When I was in school, I never paid attention to where anything was, so I don't know about Canada. I don't say anything about that, because I don't want Melvin to tell me all about Canada, wherever it is.

"Okay, well, see you tomorrow, I guess."

When I walk by Mr. Vandergriff he waves at me. I wave back and figure that's probably all I need to do right now. Before he got scared of Frankie he'd make a big point of calling me over from across the yard, and I don't feel like dealing with his son if I go over there now and he gets all freaked out again.

I wait until middle of the afternoon to call Nancy, and when she answers she says, "Hey, sweetie, how was Frankie? I didn't want to get her all excited so late and that's why I didn't come in when you invited me."

That's not what she said last night, but I figure maybe Stan or her mom is listening in, so I don't make a big deal of it.

"She's fine. Told me she'd like to see you again pretty soon."

Damn, I love to hear that girl laugh.

"Well, you tell Frankie that we'll definitely have to do that."

"I will, soon as I hang up."

We talk a little bit about H. P. and the Owlettes and Market Square and how many people were there, and it's so easy to talk to her. I'd forgotten how much I missed that. She's the one I need to talk to about

Jerry, and Momma, and Mr. Vandergriff, and all the stuff that's going on with me.

We're still just going round and round about last night and I say, "Listen, darlin', there's something I need to talk to somebody about. Can you come over here?"

"You mean right now?"

"Well, whenever. I know you've probably got stuff to do, and . . . ."

There's a short silence, and then she says, "How about tomorrow about lunchtime? I could stop somewhere and pick up some burgers or fried chicken or something."

"Sure, that sounds fine." It doesn't sound fine, but it sounds like she's not going to rush right over here just because I said so.

"I'd come over today, but Dad's got some guy from work coming for dinner and he wants us all to be there. Believe me, I would lots rather be somewhere else, but it's kind of a have to thing."

"Don't worry about it. So, tomorrow around noon?"

"Yeah. See you then."

She hangs up and I look at Frankie. "Nancy's coming over tomorrow."

I look at the clock on the stove and it's a little after three. A lot of the folks here take an afternoon nap, so there won't be anybody to talk to if I go up to the main building. Since I'm already in the kitchen, I make a sandwich and an S&S and go back into the living room. I share the sandwich with Frankie and keep the S&S for myself while I'm making sure there's nothing worth a damn on TV. Guess I'll take a nap too.

Chapter Thirteen

There's nothing on TV in the middle of the night, either, but I watch for a couple of hours anyway. After that afternoon nap I went to bed at about midnight but was up at two and it's three-thirty and I'm still awake. Since I stopped going to school, I've pretty much slept whenever I felt like it or when my S&S has been really strong. Kind of like Frankie does, except for the S&S part.

I finally give up on the TV and switch it off. I'm sitting in the dark, and there's nothing moving around outside, only a couple of lights on up at the main building, the hallways and outside the doors mainly. I can't see all the rooms, but I only see one with a light on. I wonder who that is, up in the middle of the night. Maybe they're looking down at me wondering the same thing, since I just had the TV on and there was light coming out of my window too.

I look around the little living room and something doesn't feel right. It takes me a minute to figure it out, but finally it comes to me. I'm not real smart, but even I know I'm not doing enough of any kind of work to be worth a place like this and free food too, and that makes me wonder if Carrie cooked something up with Betty when things got so bad between her and Jerry. The more I think about it the more it seems like that must have been what happened.

Daddy always told me never to take charity from anybody, said it was just a way for rich people to put themselves above the rest of us. And here I sit, in this nice house, a meal at the cafeteria whenever I want it. It's hard to call this anything else but charity.

I start thinking about all the things I want to talk to Nancy about and don't get very far before I'm dead asleep on the couch. Next thing I know it's daylight outside and Frankie's wanting either food or a trip outside. I look around, trying to figure out what to do first, and decide to head for the kitchen.

The clock on the microwave says it's 10:30. No wonder Frankie wants out. I give her some food and dump out her water dish and refill it. It takes her about a minute to clean out the food bowl, get a drink, and head for the front door. She looks back at me like, what are you waiting for?

Then she turns back to the door, alert to something outside, and a minute later there's a knock. I thought Nancy was coming by around noon, so it's probably not her. I go to the door and open it.

Tiny is standing there and doesn't say anything, just looks at me.

"Come on in, man," I say. He follows me in and plops down on the couch.

"Got any shine?" he asks. First thing he's said. No hi, how's it going, nothing.

I nod. "You want it straight?"

"Sure do," he says.

"Something going on?" I say, heading toward the kitchen. I look back and he's scratching Frankie behind the ear. He's not listening to me at all.

I bring his to him and take a drink from the one I made for myself. When I sit down on the couch Frankie looks at me for a second and then turns back to Tiny, nuzzling up under his hand.

"You're as bad as Eunuch," he says, smiling a little.

"How is Eunuch?" I say, taking a sip. That first drink was a little too big.

Tiny shrugs. "About what you'd expect with a name like that." He grins at me. "Nah, he's all right. I would've brought him with me, but I didn't know about the rules here."

"Me neither, but you bring him the next time and we'll find out," I say. "I don't think they'll give you any shit unless you let him run loose."

"I don't know, man, he's not much for being on a leash."

We sit and sip for a little while, not saying a word, and then Tiny puts his empty glass down and stands up.

"I got to go."

I take my last sip and put mine down beside his. "You sure? Seems like you just got here."

"I'd better get back. Just had to get out of the house for a while. Thanks for the shine."

He heads out the door and I hear him say, "Hey there, haven't seen you for a while," and when I step to the door he's about ten or fifteen steps away from the house and Nancy is coming toward us. She smiles at Tiny and says, "Well, you must have been hiding, then, 'cause I've been around all summer."

"I got to get back to the house. Good seeing you, Nancy."

"You, too, Tiny. Don't stay hid so long, okay?"

I get Frankie's leash on her and meet Nancy in the yard. She comes up to me and says, real low, "Is Tiny okay?"

I shrug. "Let's get back inside, darlin'. Looks like Frankie's done and it's getting warm out here."

She comes in and sees the glasses on the table. "Kind of early, isn't it?"

"He came in asking."

She frowns. "So what's going on?"

"I don't have a clue, really, he just said he needed to get out of the house for a while."

I don't know what else to say about him, so I don't say anything. She waits for me to say something else and then says, "You had lunch yet?"

I shake my head.

"Want to go get a hamburger or something?"

I start to say yes just because she asked me. Then I think, if we go somewhere we'll have to shout to hear each other and no telling who might come by the table. Nobody's going to stop to say hi to me, but everybody likes Nancy, so I figure we're pretty much guaranteed to get interrupted.

Besides that, I know I really need to talk to somebody about a lot of this stuff, and of all the people I know, she's the one I'd pick to talk to about anything.

Not that I know all that many people.

"If it's all right with you I'd just as soon stay here," I say. "I got some stuff on my mind and you're the best person I know to talk to. I just don't want to have to shout across a table in a room full of people, you know?"

Nancy looks a little disappointed, but I've got some turkey and bread and some of that cheese that's already sliced and wrapped in plastic, and plenty of Thunderstorm, so I offer to make her a sandwich and she follows me into the kitchen. I start off with Mr. Vandergriff and that sort of leads to the time Frankie scared him and that leads to Jerry.

She gets really mad when I tell her about Jerry, even when I tell her what Mark said about Jerry being in some kind of program and all that stuff about forgiveness.

"You're not going to talk to him, are you, Boone?"

When I don't answer right away she says, "I can't believe you even have to think about that."

I'm real close to telling her to mind her own damn business and then I remember that I asked her to come down here so I could talk to somebody about this stuff. I wonder when I'll ever get Daddy out of my head. Seems like every time I start to do something stupid it's exactly what he would've done. Daddy would never have felt like he needed to talk to anybody about anything, though, so at least that's different.

"He's got nothing to say I'm interested in hearing," I say, "and I'd be surprised to see him again, if you want to know the truth."

We're just about done with the sandwiches when I start talking about Momma being in Memphis and everybody pushing me to go down there and get her.

"Are you going to do it?"

"No."

"Why not? It's your mother, Boone, and she's all by herself."

Every time I hear this kind of shit it makes me mad. I'm supposed to be obligated to her and go

107

running all over the place to get her, even though she ran off and left me to Daddy when she knew how he was and then the only reason she came back was to help Jake try to steal my truck. I guess I'm not surprised that Nancy took everybody's side in this, but it still kind of pisses me off.

Neither one of us says anything for a minute, and Nancy is about to take the last bite of her sandwich when she says, kind of low, "You know, I've never seen Graceland. Or Beale Street either."

I look up at her and then away real quick, because I don't know exactly what's going on here. She's not looking at me or Frankie, just kind of off in the distance, chewing on her sandwich. She takes another drink of Thunderstorm and says, "That was a good sandwich, sweetie. Got any more Thunderstorm? And would you mind putting about three or four drops of shine in my glass before you refill it?"

I head for the kitchen with both glasses, put a few drops in hers and a medium amount in mine, put a couple of ice cubes in the glasses, and fill them both with Thunderstorm. I'm on my way back with them in my hands when there's a knock on the door and then it starts to open. Nancy and I both look toward the door and it swings in far enough for us to see Maryanne standing there. As soon as she sees us she says, "Sorry, sorry," and pulls the door shut.

Nancy looks at me when I hand her her glass. "You have a girlfriend I don't know about, Boone?"

She sounds a little mad.

"No, Maryanne just comes by once a week or so to clean the house. Guess she thought I was up at the main building."

Nancy stares at me for a second and then her mouth starts to twitch. She puts her drink down on the floor next to her feet and stares at her shoes, and her shoulders start to shake a little bit. Then she laughs out loud, and looks up at me, still laughing, and shakes her head.

She takes a breath and says, "You've got a cleaning lady," and that's all she can get out before she starts laughing again.

"Listen, darlin', she's not my cleaning lady. She works for the, I mean . . . ."

She waggles her finger at me. "I had no idea you were so rich, Boone. You should be taking me out to fancy restaurants. A cleaning lady. My, my," and she starts laughing all over again, and this time I can't help but join in.

We stay away from the serious stuff for the rest of the afternoon, and I start thinking about that money in the safe deposit box. Maybe I should be taking her out to fancy restaurants and buying her stuff. Trouble is, I don't know any fancy restaurants, except that big one we passed on the way to Knoxville, the one that has the big sign that says, "All You Can Eat Buffet" out front. Maybe I'll go there by myself first, see what it's like.

"What are you thinking about, Boone? You're a thousand miles away."

"Nothing. Just thinking about, you know, how nice it is having you around, and . . . ." I drop my head and look at the floor. I never get this kind of shit right, and I can hear how stupid I sound. I can't think of the right words or anything. I stand up and head toward the kitchen. "You want a refill?"

"Sure."

I don't look back to see what she's doing, so I don't expect her to come up behind me. She sets her glass on the counter and wraps her arms around my waist. She gives me a squeeze and says, "Maybe just a little more shine this time."

Before I know it she's looking at her cell phone and saying, "Oh my God, look at how late it is! I was supposed to help Mom cook tonight. I have to go, sweetie, sorry, but I'm already late."

She gives me a kiss that's way too short and then she's out the door. I look over at Frankie and say, "I can't believe how stupid I was to almost screw that up. She's a lot better than I deserve."

Frankie's ignoring me, staring at the door, waiting for Nancy to come back. Already.

Chapter Fourteen

After a couple of days I still haven't heard from Tiny again, so I decide to give him a call.

"Is this Boone?"

"Yes, ma'am, it is. Is Tiny around anywhere?"

"I haven't talked to you in a while, Boone. How are you doing?"

"Pretty good, Mrs. Thompson." I didn't really call to talk to her, but she's not acting like she's in any hurry to go get Tiny.

"You just missed Phillip, I'm afraid. He went into town to talk to the recruiter again."

I don't know what to say here. Tiny never said anything to me about being recruited for anything.

"Are you still there, Boone?"

"Yes, ma'am, I'm still here. Do you know about when he'll be back?"

"I don't know for sure. That Navy recruiter sure is interested in him, keeps calling here every other day or so. You want me to tell him you called?"

"If you don't mind, I'd appreciate it."

"Oh, it's no trouble at all, Boone. We need to get you up here for some ribs sometime soon. Phillip is awfully good on the grill."

"Yes, ma'am, that sounds real good."

There's a silence, and I finally say, "You take care now."

"I will, Boone. See you soon." She hangs up and I stand there staring at the phone. Navy recruiter? What the hell is Tiny doing?

He doesn't call back, and after another day I'm starting to think he's just going to take off without a word and leave me with no way to get to the still to make any more shine or even to just get my stuff and find another place to set up. I go back and forth about it, though, because it doesn't really make any sense. This is not like Tiny at all, and I'm having a lot of trouble seeing him in a uniform of any kind. Besides, he just got that dog, Eunuch. Why would he do that if he was going off to the Navy or whatever?

I decide to get lunch in the cafeteria the next day, and I go through the line and fill my plate with hamburger steak, at least that's what they call it on the little sign out in the hallway, and mac and cheese and green beans. When I get my tray filled I look around for an empty table. I spend a lot of time talking to these old folks already, and I just want to sit and eat.

I'm putting ketchup on the hamburger and the mac and cheese when somebody pulls out a chair and sits down.

"You really need to learn how to drive that Mini of mine," Mark says to me. "Want a lesson after you finish whatever's under all that ketchup? Also, you missed the green beans there."

"Couldn't find the ranch," I say. When I was in school, we used to put ranch on everything: pizza, green beans, everything. I tried it on broccoli once, but it didn't help. Nothing helps broccoli. "I didn't see any on that table with all the salt and pepper and ketchup and stuff."

"Condiments," Mark says.

"What?"

"All those things, salt, pepper, mustard, ketchup, and so on, are called condiments."

I shrug.

Mark leans toward me. "Thought any more about your mother?"

I put my fork down, hard, and push my chair back.

"If that's what you came over here to say, well, you said it. And if you're thinking to get me out in that little toy car of yours so you can talk about Momma, then you're going to be talking to yourself." I'm standing up by now and start to pick up my tray.

"Why don't you sit down and finish your plate, Boone? I won't bring it up again unless you do. Okay?"

I feel like a fool, standing there with everybody staring at me, but that hamburger steak was pretty good, the one bite I had of it, so I sit back down and say, "Long as we talk about something besides Momma. Or Jerry." I look at him. "You going to eat something?"

Mark looks again at my plate. "I might try the hamburger steak with a little less ketchup." He pushes his chair back and stands up. "Be right back."

When he gets back we eat and talk about the old folks, mostly Melvin and Mr. Vandergriff, and I tell him about the woman I saw here when Gamaliel was still alive, who might have been kin to me somehow.

He gets all interested in this and says, "Want me to try to track her down for you?"

I don't say anything, because I don't know what to say. I had never thought about it, and I wonder if she would try to get me to go to Memphis and bring Momma back.

Seems like no matter what I start talking about it always ends up being about her.

"I don't know, Mark, I'll have to let you know sometime later."

He nods, like he's been listening to me all along. He does that, it's like he understands what I've been thinking; sometimes it pisses me off and sometimes it scares me a little.

Mark points at my plate. "Finish up, Boone, and I'll take you driving. Everybody needs to know how to drive a stick."

After a half an hour I'm thinking, damn, this little thing can fly. We stay in the parking lot for the first five minutes or so, and Mark shows me where everything is and I jerk around the first few times until it starts making sense. When he tells me to take it out onto the road I get all mixed up and jerk along again for a while, but when I get it figured out and go through a couple of turns faster than that old truck could even think about doing, Mark is like, "That's how it's done, Boone!" and I'm grinning like a fool.

We don't even talk about anything but his car and I'm already dreading the thought of getting back into my truck.

When we pull into the parking lot and get out, me still about to laugh out loud I'm feeling so good, I toss Mark the keys across the top of the car, say, "You got to let me do that again, man," and turn around and Tiny is standing next to my piece of shit truck.

"I don't know how the two of you both fit inside that thing," Tiny says when Mark and I get close to him. "I know for sure I'd never be able to get behind the wheel."

"You might be surprised," says Mark. "There's a guy I know over in Nashville, where I'm from, he has one of these, and he's six-three."

"Think I'll keep my truck," Tiny says.

Mark grins at him. "You don't know what you're missing. Right, Boone?"

It still takes me a second to realize when somebody's teasing with me. I'm about to get mad at Mark for asking me to choose between his car and a pickup, then I figure out he's just playing around.

"Well, Mark, you can't haul anything bigger than Frankie in that thing, but I will admit it's fun to run the road in it. Sure does hang on through a turn." I turn to Tiny. "You know that long curve over there by the Baptist church? I was doing about forty-five through it just now."

"Bullshit," Tiny says, and now he's grinning too.

I spread my hands. "I'm just telling you."

"My word as a preacher, he was doing at least that," Mark says. "Thought I was going to have to clean out my boxers when we got back here." He slaps me on the back and says, "I have to go get ready for Sunday. Let me know when you want to try it again, Boone, and we'll stay out longer the next time."

He heads back toward the chapel and I start toward my place. When I pass Tiny I say, "You want to come in for a minute?"

Tiny spins around and takes two long steps and catches up to me. "You weren't really doing forty-five, right?"

"Hey, man, you got a preacher's word on it. Actually, I'm pretty sure it was fifty-one."

He laughs and says, "If that little thing'll do fifty through that curve I'll eat the spare tire."

Frankie's glad to see Tiny, and I realize that she's had, or I guess we've had, more company lately than we usually get in a month.

"Mom said you called," Tiny says.

"Yeah. You going into the Navy, man?"

"Well, I was," he says, and looks from Frankie up to me. "Don't guess we could have an S&S or two."

I nod. "How do you want yours?"

"Pretty damn strong, if you don't care to make it that way. At least the first one."

"I sure don't care to," I say, and fix a couple pretty damn strong.

He sits on the couch and I'm leaning against the refrigerator. The place is so small it's like we're in the same room, almost. He doesn't say anything until the drink is about half gone, then he puts it on the floor beside him and leans back.

"Like I said, I was going to join up. I really wanted out of here, and I don't know anything except how to work on the farm."

"You know cars, I mean, you got my truck going and all."

He shakes his head. "That was nothing, Boone. Your daddy didn't teach you how to take care of it, is all, and I just did the stuff you're supposed to do every now and then. I might could have torn the motor down if I had to, but I don't want to do that all day every day, you know?"

I don't say anything. I'm way behind on my S&S, so I take a drink, and then another one. Tiny leans forward and picks up his glass.

"Anyway, I thought I wanted out of here, and I figured if I went into the Army I'd end up in the desert getting my ass shot at every other day and dodging those bombs they hide in the roads over there. I figured the Navy would be better."

He takes a drink and shakes the glass at me. "I just went there one time, Boone, just once. Damn recruiter won't stop calling me."

"So you like what, changed your mind and he won't let you alone?"

"She. She won't let me alone, and Mom is so happy about me doing this I can't tell her I'm not going."

I finish my drink and grab his glass out of his hand. "You want another one?"

He nods. "That's another thing. The still."

I step into the kitchen and come back with both glasses full. "What about the still?"

I'm thinking about him being gone and me not being able to get to the still at all, or not being able to work it by myself if I could figure out how to get there without crossing Thompson land. Turns out he's thinking the same thing.

"Well, I didn't care much for that first batch we made. I mean, it was all right, but the stuff you and Gamaliel were making was a lot better. And I hate to give up on it after just one try."

"So what are you going to do about your mom?"

He shrugs. "I don't know yet. Maybe tell her they want me to be a SEAL or something."

I don't know what the hell Tiny's talking about right now.

I'm looking toward the front door and when I look back his eyes are on me.

"Don't you know what a SEAL is?"

"Sure, some kind of animal."

He laughs and I get all red in the face. I'm about to tell him to take his ass on home and leave me alone when he says, "Sorry, Boone, didn't mean to laugh out loud like that. It's a kind of Navy soldier, does the really dangerous stuff."

As soon as he says that I remember hearing about Navy SEALs; maybe I'm going at these S&S's a little fast. I nod and he keeps going.

"I know she'd worry herself sick if she thought I was going to do something like that." He's quiet for a minute, and then he says, "Maybe that's what I'll do."

I don't say anything, but I'm remembering how Momma and Hannah and I used to lie to Daddy all the time, especially when he was angry drunk, which was a lot. Wore us all out trying to keep track of what we said and when we said it, and it never made much difference anyway. He was still mad all the time and mean as a snake.

Chapter Fifteen

Before Tiny leaves he says, "So, next week we go up there and start thinking about the next batch, what measurements to change, all that stuff."

"Right."

He takes off and I think, okay, no more company for a while.

That lasts about a half an hour.

Betty is at the door. "Can I come in, Boone?"

I wonder if she can smell the shine, but I can't think of a good reason to keep her out.

"Sure, Betty, come on in. I was just getting ready to take Frankie out, get her out of the house for a while, but I can do that later."

She stops at the front door and says, "Why don't I walk with you two? I don't get enough exercise."

I know that's a lie; she is all the time walking around, checking on stuff. I don't mind, though, and it keeps her out of the house. "Sure, Betty. Frankie! Want to go for a walk?"

Frankie is at the door before I can finish, and Betty laughs and says, "Hi, Frankie, look at you! What a good girl!"

While she and Frankie are talking to each other I get the leash and snap it on. We head out toward the main building and Betty looks over at me.

"I wanted to let you know that the state inspector's coming first of next week."

I don't know what this has to do with me, don't even really know what an inspector does at an old folk's home.

"Okay, I guess. What does that mean?"

"Well, he looks at all our records and at the kitchen and dining room and all the resident's rooms to make sure we're following the law."

"So, he's like the police."

She stops and turns toward me, so I stop too. Frankie keeps going until the leash stops her and she looks back to see what the problem is.

"Not exactly, but he is from the government. There are rules we have to follow or we'll get shut down." She looks right at me. "I don't ever remember him wanting to see anything but the main building, but we've never had anybody living there where you're staying before."

I'm starting to think she's about to tell me she's found out about the shine and I have to pack up and get out.

"I'm pretty sure I saw you carrying a shotgun into the house the day you moved in," she says, "and I know that having a gun here is against the rules."

The first thing I think is, it's a good thing she doesn't know about the shine in the kitchen. The second thing is, I've got the shine, a shotgun, and Gamaliel's old rifle, and any one of them would get me kicked out of there and get Betty in trouble besides. Hell, I don't even know if it's okay that Frankie's there.

"I didn't say anything before, because you didn't have hardly anything when you got here, and I didn't want to start out by telling you to get rid of one of the few things you had," she says, "but that gun can't be in there when he is inspecting in case he wants to see inside. We can't tell him no, that would get us in trouble too, and you can't just put it in your truck, because it's still on the property."

I don't say anything.

"You should use the old maintenance road on the back of the property. Sometime this weekend, just to be on the safe side. I don't want any of our residents seeing you walking across the grounds with a shotgun. I'm awfully sorry, Boone, but it can't be helped. Do you have somebody that can hold onto it for you for a few days?"

"Can Frankie stay?"

I realize that some moonshine, a couple of guns, a few clothes, and Frankie is all I've got. It'll be a pain in the ass to hide all my stuff, but I can figure that out. If Frankie has to go, then I'm going to be looking for somewhere else to live. When I start thinking about that I can't think of anywhere to go; can't go back to our old house, it's probably fallen down already. Can't go to Gamaliel's house, Carrie and Jerry wouldn't let that happen. Can't move in with Tiny, not with all that shine to have to do something with. I'd still have to hide it somewhere like I'm getting ready to do now.

Maybe it's about time I did something with some of Gamaliel's money. I don't have any idea how much it costs to live anywhere; when Daddy was around he worked for somebody that had an old place we could use. I bet Nancy would know. Or Mark.

I look over at Betty and she's not looking at me. She's staring at the ground, and then she raises her head and I remember the last thing I said to her and say it again.

"Can Frankie stay with me? Or do I have to hide her somewhere too?"

"I heard you the first time, Boone."

"Well, you gonna answer me?" I'm starting to get mad now, because I can tell by the look on her face what she's going to say to me.

Betty looks over at Frankie and takes a deep breath.

"Mark and I have been talking about this ever since I found out the inspector was coming, trying to figure out a way to keep Frankie here at the center. We think there's a way, but you're going to have to be okay with it, and Frankie will, too."

I don't like how this sounds. Betty's real uncomfortable, and she's never like that, so I'm guessing she's cooked up some lie to tell the inspector about Frankie, and she's going to ask me to go along with it.

The thing is, I've been lying as long as I can remember. Mostly to Daddy, but not just to him. I don't think I lied to Gamaliel, but I would have if he'd asked me straight up about Daddy. Same with Nancy; I've been as honest with her as I ever have with anybody, but there's sure a couple of things I'd even lie to her about.

So as far as I'm concerned, lying to this inspector guy is nothing.

Chapter Sixteen

I'm in Mark's office the day after the inspector came snooping around, and Mark is telling me all about it.

He says Frankie was a big hit with her new collar; actually, I think Betty called it a harness, and it had "Service Animal" on both sides in bright yellow letters.

He and Betty both had said it would be better if the inspector thought that Frankie belonged to Mark, since he was on the staff and a preacher and all they really had to do was make sure that none of the old folks said anything stupid like, "Where's Boone?", so they just kept Frankie in Mark's office while the inspector went around looking at everything. I spent the day staying out of sight.

As soon as the inspector left Mark brought Frankie out into the side yard where the fountain is and all the old folks could talk about was how good-looking a dog Frankie was. I don't ask if anybody wondered where I was, because I really don't want to know. I mean, in case nobody asked.

"Yes, it worked out great. I think we've got this all figured out for the next time," Mark says.

"What are you talking about, man? What next time?"

"Well, that was the state representative for the people in Nashville who issue certificates, you know, so we can stay open. There's also the fire inspector, the kitchen inspector, and ADA, and I'm sure I'm forgetting somebody."

"So I'm going to have to hide out over and over again? And clean out my house? How often do these guys show up, anyway?"

He frowns a little. "I don't think that'll happen often, Boone. We'll ask Betty, of course, but I think the fire inspector is going to look at the alarm system and make sure everybody can walk, you know, so they can get out. The kitchen inspection shouldn't have anything to do with you. We'll see. I'm sure it's not going to be every time somebody wants to come look at the place."

"Well," I say.

I don't really believe him, but I pretend like I do. I think now that it's okay to tell me to go off and hide somewhere, it's all over. Next time it'll be some rich asshole that wants to put his momma here and it'll be, "Boone, why don't you go see Nancy tomorrow?" or something like that. I know how this goes.

Momma used to say that, a lot. "Well," she'd say, and we all knew what it really meant. It meant that we were wrong, or stupid, or full of shit, or something, and she was too polite to say so.

I've pretty much stopped listening to Mark even though he's still talking. When I start listening again he's talking about Jerry.

"You know, sooner or later he'll be back around, Boone, and you're going to have to deal with him," Mark says.

"I got nothing to say to him," I say, "and I don't want to hear anything he has to say to me."

"Maybe not," Mark isn't looking at me. He's looking around his office. "I don't see it right now, but I think I know what he was talking about when he told you he needed to make amends. I think maybe he needs to talk to you."

"Well, Mark, if that making amends thing means make up for what he did to me I don't think he's got enough time left to do that."

Mark shakes his head. "You're a hard man to be so young, Boone. I hope you can give him a chance. Even if you're sure he wouldn't give you one. Maybe especially if he wouldn't."

"It's not Sunday, man, don't start preaching to me."

He grins. "I can't help it, Boone, it's in my blood."

I don't grin back. It doesn't matter to me what Jerry needs, if I were to go the rest of my life without seeing him again that would be just fine.

Mark looks like he's getting ready to say something else, so I stand up and say, "I got to go, Mark, you know, move back in."

"I didn't know you had all that much to move out," he says, sounding a little puzzled.

That was a stupid thing to say, about moving back in. I start to make up some kind of lie about it, but I can't think of any lie that would work. So I'm standing there and it looks like Mark is getting ready to ask me a question, then his face changes and he grins at me.

"Anything to get out of here, right, Boone?"

I grin back at him. I guess I didn't even think about telling him the truth.

"Go on," he says, still grinning.

"C'mon, Frankie," I say, and we head out the side door into the space between the chapel and the main building. We go down to the house and I start to take off Frankie's fancy harness and then decide to leave it on for a while. We both know she's good for the old folks; they really like seeing her, more than me for sure. Maybe being here's not so much charity after all, even though it's Frankie that's really got the job here. I'm just along for the ride.

After I make a sandwich for me and fill Frankie's bowl, I get the keys to the truck and say, "Want to go for a ride, girl? We've got some stuff to pick up and bring back here."

She's at the door already, and I take off the harness and we go up to the parking lot. On the way I see Betty and start to tell her I'm going to be coming onto the back of the property with the truck, and then stop. What if she has decided that I can't bring my guns back into the house?

We get into the truck and sit there for a minute. Would it be better to go now and get the shine and the guns, while it's still daylight? More people are going to see me now, but if I wait I'll have to use the headlights and somebody will sure notice if there's headlights bouncing around on that back road into the place. Daylight's probably best. We pull out of the parking lot on the way to pick up the guns and the shine.

We stop at the first stand of trees off the state road on the way to the old wreck of a house I first saw when Nancy was taking me for that drive. The shine's up there in the house, but I figured if whoever was using that place for a meth house came back I'd rather them just get the shine and not the guns too.

"You stay here, Frankie," I say and hop out. The shotgun and Gamaliel's old rifle are just a little ways back in the woods, wrapped in an old tarp and laid on a couple of branches of a dogwood tree. They're still there, like I thought they would be. Chances of somebody coming through that part of the woods and looking up into the branches instead of where they were stepping were pretty small, especially since it had only been two days. I'm more worried about all that shine. If whoever was using that old place came back through it'd be hard not to notice the jars sitting in the corner of the room.

We spend a little time there letting Frankie run. She doesn't get much of a chance to do that, and there's plenty of light left. I get the shine loaded in the back of the truck and covered up and I'm just about to call for her when I hear a shotgun close by and, right after that, I hear Frankie coming toward me through the brush.

She breaks out into the open and she's limping bad. I run to her and grab her up and run back to the truck, throw her in the passenger seat, and take off like a bat out of hell.

How I keep from turning over those jars I'll never know, because I'm not paying any attention to anything except staying on the road and getting to the vet. We pull into the Binfield Vet Clinic and I scoop her up into my arms and run into the lobby. The staff there takes one look at me and Frankie and one of them comes around the counter and takes her out of my arms and heads back through the double doors, and I can hear her calling for the vet.

I'm standing there and I look down at my shirt. There's blood on it, seems like a lot.

Some son of a bitch shot my dog.

All of a sudden I'm dizzy and I turn around and head back out to the truck and lean against the side. My arms are crossed and I'm looking into the truck bed and a couple of the jars are showing out from under the tarp. I reach over and pull the tarp back over them and then I'm bent double by the side of the truck, puking my guts out.

I'm wiping my mouth with the back of my hand when the vet, the old guy, comes out the door and looks around. When he sees me he hurries over.

"It's Boone, right? You're Frankie's owner?"

I nod.

"First thing is, she's going to be okay. She caught some shotgun pellets in her right rear leg, but no bones are broken and I think we got all the pellets out. Dr. Kempson is finishing up and checking to make sure we didn't miss anything. I knew you'd want to know that Frankie's going to be all right. We're going to keep her here overnight, okay? You come by tomorrow at the end of the day and pick her up and we'll go over what we did and how you can take care of her, when to bring her back in, and so on. Okay?"

I nod again. I'm too wiped out to even say thank you or anything.

He pats me on the shoulder. "You go home and change, get out of those clothes. She's a strong dog, looks like you take good care of her. She's going to be fine. You go on home now, you hear?"

He pats me again. "I've got to go back inside. I'll check with Dr. Kempson and we'll get her settled, and I've got a surgery this afternoon I have to get ready for. Don't worry, Boone."

He turns around and disappears through the clinic door. I stand there for a minute and then get in the truck and turn toward the old folk's home.

I'm heading toward the parking lot like usual and then I remember what I've got in the bed of the truck. I turn off just before the entrance and drive down the back of the property, park the truck, and unload. When I get back to the parking lot and get out, I make it about halfway across the lot when Mark sees me. He's getting ready to get into his car, but he's close enough to see the blood on my shirt and he runs across the lot. Fastest I've ever seen him move.

"What the hell happened to you?"

I start laughing and can't stop. I just stand there like a fool wearing this bloody shirt laughing my ass off. Finally I get my breath.

"You cuss like that a lot, Mark?"

He pays no attention to my question at all. "Are you okay, Boone? Of course you're not okay, you're all bloody. Oh my God, where's Frankie? Is Frankie okay? Will you tell me what happened?"

He's looking in the truck and in the bed and all around where I parked. "Where's Frankie, Boone? Do I need to go get her or anything?"

When I reach out to grab him and try to slow him down, I see that my hand is trembling. Mark sees it too and takes my arm. "Come on into my office, Boone, and sit down, okay?"

I let him lead me across the lot and down the side of the building to the door closest to his office. When we step inside Maryanne is standing in the hallway. She takes one look at me and is getting ready to scream and Mark says in that preacher's voice, the one he uses when he's saying something important, "He's all right, Maryanne. Don't upset the residents. Go get Betty and tell her I need her in my office. You understand? Don't talk to anybody else. Boone's okay. Just go get Betty."

She nods and takes off, and Mark and I go into his office.

"Sit down, Boone. Are you hurt? Is that your blood?"

"No, Mark, it's Frankie's. She's okay, I got her to the vet. I got to go get her tomorrow."

I've been sitting in one of his chairs, my elbows on my knees, looking at the floor. Now I raise my head and look right at Mark.

"I took Frankie out for a run up at an old house nobody lives in anymore, and some son of a bitch shot her with a shotgun."

"You mean on purpose, Boone? What kind of evil person would do that?"

I'm so mad and scared for Frankie I can hardly think straight, but finally I shake my head. "No, probably not on purpose. I don't know. I don't know. It's not even the season for anything. Maybe some kid with a new gun just trying it out, shooting at nothing, you know? I mean, if they were trying to shoot her they're a really shitty shot."

Mark nods.

"I know I'm going to find whoever it was and kick his ass, I know that." I've been holding my left hand with my right and when I let go, I'm still trembling. I grab my left hand again.

Betty comes in right then, doesn't knock or anything.

"Boone, what the hell happened to you?"

Chapter Seventeen

I just sit there while Mark tells Betty what he knows, and then I feel a hand on my shoulder. I start to jerk away, but I don't, and then I'm shaking all over and tears are falling on my hands and Mark's got his arm around me holding on real tight and Betty is crouched down in front of me holding both of my hands and I look up and her eyes are wet and the tears are starting down her cheeks.

"Mark said you told him she's going to be okay, Boone," she says, and her voice is whispery and soft and I nod. She squeezes my hands and then stands up. Mark's still got a hold of me and I don't pull away from him.

I can feel my breathing settle down and eventually he lets go and goes around to his desk. He says, "Betty, I'll be back in a minute. Can you stay here with him?"

"Of course I can."

The door opens and closes, and a minute later opens again.

"Okay, Betty, I'm going to take Boone back down to his house so he can change. We'll go around the outside so we won't have to answer any questions about his shirt or anything."

She nods her head and Mark takes hold of my arm. I stand up and Betty throws her arms around me and hugs me real tight, like she never does, and says, "I'm so thankful, Boone, I'm just thankful." Then she steps back and looks down at her front and sees the blood. Most of the blood on my shirt was dried but there's a few pretty good sized spots on her now and she says, "Damn. Look at me; I'll have to get Maryanne to walk in front of me to get me to my office. I think I've got a sweatshirt there I can put on."

Mark laughs and says, "I don't know, Betty, I think maybe red's your color."

We both stare at him, and then Betty smiles just a little. Then she laughs out loud. "Do you think so?" she asks.

He nods. "I do."

"I'm still going to get Maryanne to walk in front of me," she says, and picks up Mark's desk phone. She punches a button and says, "Maryanne, could you come to Mark's office? Thank you."

Mark and I slip out the side door and I turn to see Maryanne heading down the hall. She's in a hurry, like she thinks she's in trouble or something.

"Come on, Boone," says Mark.

When we get to the house and go inside, I go pick up Frankie's water bowl because that's what I always do and then I just stand there like a fool with the bowl in my hand. Mark takes it from me and puts it back on the floor. "We'll fill that up tomorrow when we go get her, so she can have some fresh water," he says. "Why don't you go change?"

I go back into the bedroom and strip off the shirt. I drop it on the floor and pick up a shirt from the pile on the bed and pull it over my head. It sounds like Mark is talking to me but I can't make out what he's saying.

"You got to talk louder, man, I can't hear you," I say.

There's no answer and then Nancy comes through the bedroom door and grabs me, hard, and says, "I came as soon as Mark called me, Boone, I am so sorry! She's going to be okay, right?, that's what Mark said. I got here as soon as I could."

She's still holding on so tight I can't hardly breathe, but I don't care. I guess I didn't hear the door when she came in the house.

"Is Mark gone?" I finally say.

She nods. "He let me in and then went back up to his office. He said to come get him if you need anything."

She lets go and takes me by the hand. "Come on in here and sit down, okay?"

I follow her into the living room and she sits down on the couch and pulls me down beside her. "What happened, Boone? Where were you when, you know, when it happened?"

"You know that old abandoned house we saw last year sometime? It's on the state road that heads toward the interstate. You told me that you hadn't seen anybody there in a long time." She's looking at me and doesn't say anything. "Well, I was letting Frankie run, you know, she doesn't get to do that unless I'm up at Tiny's, and I was about ready to head back here and that's when she got hit."

"Who was it? Did you see anybody?"

"No, I don't know. I didn't see anybody, no cars or anything around there, and I didn't hear anybody moving around. Guess I wasn't paying attention."

I don't say anything else but I'm thinking, I almost lost her today, a little more and she'd have got it right in the side. Damn stupid place to hide all that shine, but I don't have any other place. I'm all the time living off of somebody else, and I hate it. I hate it.

"What is is you hate, sweetie?"

I must've been saying that last out loud.

I just shake my head.

"I know you hate it that Frankie's not here, but that clinic's taken care of our pets for years and they're really good there. They'll take good care of her, Boone, I know they will. She'll be okay, and I'll come with you tomorrow to pick her up. Okay?"

I look up at her and she's staring right at me. I nod once, and then take a deep breath. "I know, darlin', I know she's going to be okay. I'll sure be glad when tomorrow gets here."

And that's all I can think of to say. I don't want to get into the rest of it, because there's no way she could understand that part. She has a house and a family, hell, her brother is still alive, and she's going off to college soon. That makes me think of something.

"When are you going off to school?"

"Not for another six or eight weeks. Why?"

"Just that I won't see much of you after that, and I was wondering."

She smacks me on the shoulder. "That's not true, because you're going to come down and see me a lot. I already know which dorm I'm staying in."

"You're not going to live at home?"

She doesn't say anything, and after a minute I look over at her. She's staring at the floor.

"Right now let's just worry about Frankie, okay?"

Nancy stays with me for another hour or two and then goes on back home, At the door she gives me a long kiss and then leans back to look up at me.

"You call me when you get ready to go pick her up, okay?"

One more hug and she's gone.

This place feels sad and empty without Frankie here. TV's no good, the S&S I fix doesn't taste right, and I try the couch and then the bed and then the couch again and can't get comfortable anywhere. I finally fall asleep on the couch and get a really awful night's sleep.

When I wake up I look around for Frankie just like I always do and then remember what happened yesterday. It's six in the morning, and I never get up this early. I eat half a bowl of cereal and call the vet, and get a recording telling me they'll be open at eight. Still an hour and a half from now. Any other day I'd still be asleep. Most mornings I get up at eight or nine or ten, whenever. Wish I could go back to sleep, but I know that's not going to happen.

I go up to the parking lot to get the truck. It needs gas, and I got nothing else to do right now but wait on the vet to open. It smokes just a little when I start it up and I think, I need to remember to ask Tiny about that. The drive to the gas station is short, but long enough to remind me that I'm not driving Mark's little car. Damn, that thing was a lot of fun.

When I get back I start toward the house, but as I turn the corner I hear somebody call me.

"Boone, is that you?"

Melvin's sitting in his regular place, waving at me to come over. I don't feel like talking to anybody, but I don't like how the house feels without Frankie in it. I head toward him and as soon as I get close he says, "Where's Frankie?"

"She's at the vet."

"Is everything okay?"

I look at him like he's a damn fool to ask that question, and then remember that most people here don't know about what happened.

"Boone? You okay, son?"

"You're not my damn daddy."

Right away I wish I hadn't said that, but I can't take it back, and I keep looking at the ground.

"I know that, Boone."

When I raise my head up to look at him, he's leaning toward me a little and looking me right in the eye.

"Sorry, Melvin, I shouldn't've said that."

He doesn't say anything, and I can't keep looking at him, so I look back down at the ground.

It's real quiet; nobody else is out this early, and neither one of us says anything for a long time.

Finally I can't stand it anymore and I say, "Somebody shot Frankie. She's at the vet, and they're not open yet, so I can't check on her."

I'm afraid if I say anything else I'll start crying like a little kid, so I just stand there.

"Why don't you sit down, Boone? I won't ask any more questions, I promise."

He doesn't say anything else, and I stand there for another minute and then sit down.

He's kind of like Gamaliel, I think. Not exactly; in some ways he's nothing like the old man. I never saw Gamaliel with a book in his hand, and Melvin's always got three or four next to him on the bench or in his lap, and he's always talking about stuff I've never heard before.

But he's easy to be with, like Gamaliel was. The old man used to give me shit all the time, but I never minded it, which is strange now that I think about it. Gamaliel would say stuff to me and call me out on stuff that from anybody else would have gotten me up on my feet or out the door. Melvin doesn't go that far, but it's hard for me to think about getting up and walking off from him or telling him to stay out of my damn business. Most grownups I'd rather not be around, but Gamaliel was different, and seems like Melvin is too.

Then I think about what Nancy said, about me being eighteen and all, and I guess that makes me a grownup too. I sure as hell don't feel like one.

"Don't feel like one what, Boone?"

I have got to stop doing that. I talk to Frankie all the time and don't ever worry about what I say. She's not going to ask me about it later or repeat it to anybody else, and I guess I must have said part of what I was thinking just now out loud.

"Nothing, Melvin. Listen, I got to go."

I stand up and Melvin says, "Where are you going? Is Frankie ready to be picked up?"

I'd forgotten all about it being too early to call the vet. I was all ready to go get my dog.

"Oh, yeah. Guess it's too early yet to call and check on her. They told me I could pick her up today, but I'm supposed to call first to make sure."

"What time do they open?"

"Eight, I think."

He looks at his watch. "You want to go to the cafeteria and get some breakfast?"

"I had a bowl of cereal already."

Melvin shakes his head. "How long has it been since you had an omelet?"

I don't answer. Momma never fixed omelets; I can't remember breakfast being much of a meal. We were lucky to get eggs once or twice a month. Mostly it was cereal, and about half the time I wouldn't eat anything at all.

"They don't always have omelets, but they have eggs and bacon and biscuits every day. I haven't eaten myself, usually come out here to read for a while when the weather's nice. I was thinking about going in when I saw you. Why don't you join me? It'll take your mind off Frankie for a few minutes, and then it'll be time to call the vet."

Chapter Eighteen

Breakfast is awful. The food is okay, better than cereal, but everybody keeps coming over to where Melvin and I are sitting and asking where Frankie is. I have to say the same thing over and over again, and I'm getting madder and madder all the time. Pretty soon it doesn't matter how good the food is, I just want out of here and away from all these people.

Melvin's looking more unhappy all the time, too, and finally he says, "I'll take care of the dishes, Boone. Why don't you get out of here? I thought this would be a good idea. Guess I was wrong."

I'm about half mad at Melvin for asking me to come in here, so I just get up and leave.

When I get back to the house it's almost eight o'clock, so I turn on the TV and go through the channels a couple of times. There isn't anything worth a damn on, like usual, but it takes up time, and by the second look at everything that's on, it's a minute or two after eight.

I call the vet and they put me on hold. After what seems like a long time Dr. Kempson says, "Is this Boone?"

"Yeah. How's Frankie?"

"She's good. I checked on her as soon as I got in, just a few minutes ago, and I'm not seeing anything that worries me."

I don't think I knew how worried I was until right this minute. Even though they told me yesterday that Frankie was going to be okay, after not having her here all night I guess I was pretty scared.

"So when can I pick her up?"

"Well, I'd feel a lot better if we could keep an eye on her until the end of the day. How about 4:00? That's just before we close."

I start to say not a chance in hell, I'm coming to get my dog, and then I think that maybe I ought to let them make sure she's all right.

"Okay, see you around four."

"She's a strong dog, Boone, she's going to be fine."

"Okay."

I know I'm repeating myself, but I'm already thinking that I need to call Nancy and also let Mark and Betty know. And Melvin. And I can't think of any questions to ask, so I say, "Listen, thanks, doc," and he says he'll talk to me more this afternoon.

My first call is to Nancy, and she doesn't pick up, so I head out the door to find Mark.

Mark is in the hallway outside his office talking to Mr. Vandergriff, so I hang back a little ways. Mr. Vandergriff is doing all the talking, which is the way he was sometimes with me, and Mark is nodding his head and looking like it's the most interesting stuff he's ever heard. I have to do that sometimes with these old folks, but I can't keep it up for more than a minute or two before I'm looking for a way out. I guess Mark has to do this a lot, being a preacher.

Mr. Vandergriff catches me in the corner of his eye and looks around. He's checking to see if Frankie's with me, I know. I don't think he ever got over being scared when Jerry showed up that time and Frankie started growling down low like she does.

"Where's your dog, Boone?"

"Frankie's at the vet, Mr. Vandergriff."

He nods. Doesn't ask me about how she is or anything. Just turns back to Mark and says, "Now where was I?"

Mark is looking at his watch. "Actually, Eliot, why don't we finish this at, say, 10:30? I've got some free time then."

Mr. Vandergriff grumbles a little bit and then says okay. Mark pats him on the shoulder and says, "I'll come find you at 10:30."

Then he looks at me and tilts his head toward his office door. "See you later, Eliot," he says, and goes into his office.

When we're both inside he closes the door and shakes his head. "That man does love to talk. But you knew that already."

I don't say anything.

Mark points toward a chair and moves around behind his desk. "Any word on Frankie?"

He sits down and I do too. "Yeah, I thought you'd want to know. I'm supposed to pick her up at four this afternoon."

"Not until then? Is she all right?"

"The vet says yes, he just wants to keep an eye on her until the end of the day."

"That is really good news, Boone. Thank the Lord she's okay."

I nod. I don't say anything because I'm getting all teary again. I don't know what it is about this room, seems like half the time I'm in here I'm crying about something.

"So what are you going to do until then?"

"Well, I haven't got hold of Nancy yet, so I've got to call her. And find Betty."

Mark says, "I'll be talking to Betty in," he looks at his watch again, "about ten minutes. Want me to tell her?"

"Sure."

I stand up. "I thought you'd want to know about Frankie, Mark. I'm going to try Nancy again and then get out of here."

He points to the phone on his desk. "Try her now if you want."

This time I get her and she says, "I'll be at your place at 3:30 so I can go with you. I'm so glad she's all right, sweetie. See you then?"

"Sounds good," I say, and after she's gone I turn to Mark. "I'll see you later."

"Where are you going, Boone?"

I should say none of your business, but I don't.

"I'm going back up to where she got shot."

Mark frowns. "Why would you want to do that?"

"I'm going to look for the son of a bitch that shot Frankie. If I find him I'm going to kick his ass."

"That's a bad idea, Boone. You know it very likely wasn't on purpose."

I'm already opening the door. "Well, then, he needs a lesson on how not to make that kind of mistake again."

He starts to say something else, but by then I'm at the outside door.

No smoke this time when I start up the truck, which is good. I pull out onto the road and fifteen minutes later I'm looking at that house that's about to fall in on itself. I roll down the window and turn off the engine. It's quiet here, far enough away from the roads that I have to listen hard to hear the traffic. There's no breeze, so the trees are quiet too.

I open the door and step out. Still nothing, not even a bird singing. Then I hear a screech and look up. Way off over the roof of the house I can see a hawk making a lazy circle just above the trees. It drifts off out of sight and I hear it once more and then it's gone.

The woods come up close to the old house but there's twenty or thirty feet of open space all around it. I make the circle and there's nothing except just a touch of wind every now and then that bends the grass a little and waves the smallest branches on the trees at the edge of the clearing.

For a few minutes I stand still and let the quiet soak into me. There's almost nothing I miss about where I used to live; Momma was always scared, Daddy was usually drunk or mad or both, and I usually hated being there. The woods behind the house, though, I guess I do miss that. There's no place like this around where I'm living now. I'm starting to think about how nice it would be if Frankie was here, or, better yet, Nancy and Frankie both, when I hear the shotgun.

It's far off, up the ridge behind me and to my left. I turn that way and start to head into the woods and then stop. I'm not sure enough of where it came from to keep going. I need at least one more shot to get my direction set. I wait and wait, and there's nothing. Just that one blast, and I know it came from up on the ridge, but it was pretty far off and I'm not sure, I'm just not sure.

"Hey!" I yell in the general direction of where I think it came from. "Hey! There's people down here! Stop your damn shooting!"

Nothing. No answer, no noise of people moving through the brush, nothing.

"You the guy that shot my dog, asshole? Come on down here, I'll kick your ass for you!"

As peaceful as I was two minutes ago, I'm so mad I'm trembling now. Frankie's hurt and I can't fix her and I can't get to the guy that did it.

Still nothing.

I go around the house so fast I'm almost running, stopping and listening and then moving again. On the far side of the house from the truck I catch a briar branch right across my forehead and I start bleeding down into my eyes. That pisses me off even more, but it also slows me down some. I go back to the truck and get up into the seat. When I turn the rear view mirror to look at my face I can see three scratches across my forehead. They don't look deep and they're only about two or two and a half inches long, but it's a scalp wound, which means I'm bleeding like a stuck pig.

There's no more shooting going on and I'm already in the truck, so I start it up and turn around in the yard. I drive back out to the road and start back towards home, driving with one hand and pushing on my forehead with the other. I'm about halfway home when I see the blue lights in the side mirror. I'd forgotten to move the rear view back into place. I have to go another hundred yards to find the first wide place in the road to pull over; I'm hoping he's after somebody else and just wants me out of the way. He pulls in right behind me, so I guess it was me.

It's Deputy Anderson. He comes up on the driver's side and taps on the window. I'm rolling it down when he sees the blood on my face and says, "You need to step on out of the car now."

I get out and he says, "Okay, I thought that was you, Boone. What the hell happened to your face?"

"Hi, Deputy Anderson. I got smacked by a briar branch, looking the wrong way, I guess. It's not bad, just bleeding a lot."

"Let me see it."

I drop my hand and he looks, then reaches out and touches my forehead. "You're right, it's pretty shallow. Come on back here."

He leads me to the back of his car and opens the trunk. He takes out a first aid kit, opens that, and pulls on a pair of those doctor's gloves. There's a roll of paper towels in the trunk, too, and he tears off a couple and dabs around on my head, then looks at the cuts. He unrolls some gauze and tears off a few strips of tape and covers the cuts, tapes them up, and then steps back. "That should get you back home. You look like hell, but you're not bad hurt."

I nod. "Thanks, I appreciate it."

He grins. "You were weaving a little and when you pulled over I noticed you have a taillight out. Didn't know I was going to be doing any first aid. So where were you moving so fast that you didn't notice that briar?"

I tell him about what happened to Frankie and about going back up there this morning and hearing the shotgun. He's watching me the whole time and when I stop talking he says, "While you were telling that story you were getting madder and madder. I think maybe it's a good thing you didn't find whoever was shooting."

He starts back toward his door and then turns. "That was a damn fool thing to do, by the way, chasing off like that. Did anybody even know where you were?"

I say that Mark did, but that isn't entirely true, since Mark has no idea where that house is.

Deputy Anderson shakes his head. "Still a foolish move. Could have gotten your ass shot, you know."

I start to tell him he can't talk to me like that, but I'm thinking he's right. It was pretty stupid.

Next time I'll take my own gun, I say to myself, and then think, that's about the only thing that would make what I did stupider.

Chapter Nineteen

When I get back I go straight down to my house. I don't want anybody to see me with this stuff all over my forehead. I yank the tape off and have a look in the mirror. They're still bleeding a little, but nothing like before, and I wash all the dried blood off my face and put on a clean shirt.

Betty is out in the side yard and when I go up to her she looks at me and says, "The supply closet is down the same hall as Mark's office, on the other side. There should be a box of bandaids in there. Looks like a briar caught you in the face."

"Yeah, that's exactly what happened. I just wasn't paying attention."

She shakes her head. "Go on, it's not bleeding bad, but you ought to get it taken care of. Mark told me about Frankie. That's great news, Boone. You're going to get her this afternoon?"

I nod and say, "Sure missed her last night."

"I'll bet."

She turns back to the woman she was talking to; it's somebody I don't know. Probably just moved in.

Maryanne is opening the closet door when I come down the hallway.

"Mr. Boone, what happened to your face?"

She's talking to me, but she's looking around for Frankie.

"Frankie's at the vet, Maryanne."

"Oh. Is she okay?"

"Yeah, I'm supposed to pick her up this afternoon." I don't feel like going over what happened one more time, and she doesn't push.

"You need a bandage. Here, let me get it for you."

She gets out a big roll of gauze and I say, "Is that all you've got?"

"What do you mean?"

"I was thinking a bandaid or two would take care of it."

"Oh." She looks at my forehead and then in the box of bandaids on the shelf next to the door. "How about this one?"

She holds up a bandaid.

"Yeah, that's good. Better give me three or four."

She gets three more and says, "Step over here, next to the door."

"Why?"

"The light is better. I'll go ahead and put them on for you."

"Oh. Okay, I guess."

I'm not all that tall, but I have to lean down a little. Maryanne opens a couple of them and starts to put the first one on, then stops and digs a tissue out of her pocket. She wipes my forehead and then puts both bandaids on. I straighten up and she says, "I think that will do for now. Here, Mr. Boone, you take these," and she gives me a handful, "just in case you need them later."

"Thanks."

"You are welcome." She hurries off down the hall, back to the closet.

"She's really pretty, isn't she?"

I look around and Mark is standing there.

I shrug.

"Don't give me that, Boone, I saw how you were watching her. Don't do anything stupid, now. You just got things back in good shape with Nancy."

"I know that." I got to say, she is a good-looking woman. Mark's right, I know he's right.

"Besides," I say, "she's scared of Frankie, so it'd never work out anyway."

Mark is looking right at me. "I'm not kidding, Boone. You're a smart guy. Don't forget to act like one."

Then he grins. "So, before you go get Frankie, you want to go for another ride?"

"What time is it?"

He looks at his watch. "Not quite 11. You've got plenty of time. Come on, I'll buy you a hamburger in town."

The car is just as much fun as I remember it being. Mark lets me drive the whole way there, and we're a little early for lunch, so there's a lot of empty tables.

"So, did you go there this morning?"

"Yeah."

He says, "I thought that might be how you got those cuts on your face." He dips a French fry into the pile of ketchup on his plate and waves it at me. "You're a smart kid, Boone. It worries me when you forget that."

"I'm not a kid." I sure don't need a lecture from a preacher right now.

"Oh, that's right. You had the magic birthday. Well, then, you're a smart young man. It still worries me when you forget to act like one."

Mark doesn't have any idea what a mess I made of school, and I'm not about to tell him that. He sure doesn't know whether I'm smart or not, and it kind of feels funny, him calling me that. I know it's not true, and it makes me think he's after something.

I take another bite of my hamburger, and Mark pops the fry into his mouth.

He takes a sip of his drink and says, "You need any money for the vet?"

I hadn't even thought about that. I guess I need to go by the bank. I'm sure Gamaliel wouldn't mind me using some of that money to take care of Frankie.

"I don't think so. Reckon how much it might be?"

Mark spreads his hands. "It's always more than you think it's going to be, Boone. You sure you don't need any?"

"No, I'm good." I take the last bite of the burger and finish off my drink. The fries were gone about halfway through the meal. This place makes those really skinny fries, and I could eat a bucket full easy.

"You ready?"

"One more bite," says Mark. "I like to enjoy my food, and besides, I've got paperwork when we get back." He takes another sip. "Did you see the new resident? She's only been here a week or so. I don't know very much about her, but you might introduce yourself when you get a chance. We're getting a good collection of stories, and a new source is always welcome."

"Okay," I say. I've been thinking that Melvin probably has a bunch of good stories he hasn't told me yet, but I'll check out this new person and see what she's got to say.

Mark stands up. "Let's get out of here. Toss me the keys; I want to drive on the way back. There's a great road I want to show you. It'll make the trip back a little longer, but my car just loves it."

I call Nancy when I get back. "Is there any way you can come at 3:00 instead of 3:30? I need to stop somewhere."

She's there a few minutes before 3:00. "So where are we going?"

"I got to stop by the bank. Don't know how much it's going to cost, but I know I'll have to pay them something."

She says, "Why don't you just write them a check?"

I haven't told her about Gamaliel's money. Actually I haven't told anybody, and I'm thinking maybe I should tell her. Nancy may be the only person I really trust.

"I'd feel better with cash in my hand."

"Well, okay, but that's why people have checking accounts. So they won't have to carry around a bunch of cash money."

I shrug. "We'd better get going."

On the way to the bank I keep touching the safety deposit box key and Nancy finally says, "The vet already told you Frankie was going to be all right. I swear, you're like a little kid in church, squirming around over there."

We're in Nancy's car because my truck doesn't have a back seat and I want Frankie to be comfortable, not jammed between us the whole way back. She turns into the bank parking lot and shuts

161

off the car. I turn to her and say, "I want you to come in with me."

"Why? Just so you can cash a check?"

I really don't know what to do here. If I show her the money, she might, hell, she might do a lot of things. She might faint dead away right there in the bank, or tell me I need to give it to Carrie, or who knows what. I'm sure she won't say that Jerry should get it, but past that I just don't know.

Then I decide, what the hell.

"No, so I can show you what's in the safety deposit box."

She turns in the seat to face me. "What are you talking about?"

I figure I'd better tell her before we get in there instead of pulling out a box full of cash. So I tell her the whole thing, how Gamaliel wanted me to clear out the drawers next to his favorite chair and about finding the gun and the box of money, and how he told me that he wanted me to have it when he was gone, and to keep it away from Jerry no matter what.

"How much money are we talking about here?"

"I don't know, maybe eighteen thousand or so. I never did count it all out, just, you know, after you helped me get started with the bank, I decided it would be better there, I mean here. You remember when Jake stole my truck? The box of money was behind the seat. I almost lost it then and I figured I'd better not take any more chances with it."

Nancy is staring at me with her mouth a little open.

"I mean, I still kind of think it's Gamaliel's money, even though he's gone, you know? I think he'd be okay with me using some of it for Frankie, though."

Nancy starts laughing and pretty soon she can't get her breath, she's laughing so hard. I don't see anything funny about this, and I'm about to tell her so when she kind of shakes herself and says, "You have almost twenty thousand dollars?"

I nod.

"Twenty. Thousand."

I nod again.

"And you haven't spent any of it?"

"Like I said, it still feels like it's his money. I know it's stupid, but I can't help it."

She's back to staring at me.

"So how much do you think the vet'll cost?" I say. She's not thinking about the vet, I can tell that. She's just staring.

"You have all that money, and you . . . you . . ."

She looks down and then back up at me. "I don't understand, Boone, really I don't. You could be buying nice things."

"Like what?"

"Well, like clothes, or a new truck, or, well, you know."

"I'm trying to tell you, I never called it my money. I was saving it."

"For what?"

I start to say, in case Gamaliel needs it, and catch myself. Really, I don't know for what.

"Listen, can we talk about this some other time? I need to go get Frankie."

"Of course we can," she says, "but we are definitely going to talk about this."

"So, how much do you think the vet will cost?"

"I don't have any idea, sweetie, but surely if you take two hundred dollars you'll be fine."

We go into the bank and into the little room where all the boxes are. I hand over my key and they use their key and mine to unlock the box, take it to the table in the middle of the room, and then they're gone. It's just me and Nancy.

Man, I hate to do this. I'm thinking once I start spending Gamaliel's money it'll get easier and easier. But I need to get my dog back, so I open the box and Nancy looks inside.

"Oh, my God, Boone, you were serious! Look at all that damn money!" She realizes how loud she's being and looks around real quick, her hand over her mouth.

"Did you think I was lying to you?" I don't like it much that it sounds like she didn't believe me out in the car.

She shakes her head and then uncovers her mouth. "No, sweetie, no, that's not it. It's just a lot of money. More than I've ever seen in one place."

I grin at her. "That's what I thought when I opened the box at Gamaliel's house."

"Twenty thousand dollars. My boyfriend's rich." She's smiling.

She picks up one of the rolls of bills and cuts her eyes at me, still smiling. Then her face changes and she says, "Sorry, sorry," and puts it back in the box. She takes a step back. "We ought to go get Frankie, don't you think?"

Chapter Twenty

Something went wrong back there in the bank, but I'll be damned if I know what it is. Nancy's driving real fast and not looking at me at all. We pull into the parking lot at the vet's and she turns to me and says, "Just so you know, I wasn't going to take any of your precious money."

"What are you talking about?" I know I didn't say anything, not even when she picked up that roll and pretended to put it in her pocket.

"Oh, the look on your face was pretty clear, Boone. You don't need to worry, though. It's all locked up in your vault. I'll give you your key back as soon as we get your dog. We'll go right to my house and — "

I start to reach over to her and she shies away from me. How I can screw things up so fast I don't know, but I sure have screwed this up. I don't know what to say, and I'm afraid I'll say the wrong thing.

"Look at you, Boone, you're all slumped down in the seat. You're like a whipped dog."

I heard that kind of shit from Daddy all the time, and I'll be damned if I'm going to take it from anybody else, not even Nancy. I'm feeling like if I don't get out of the car right now, it's going to be the peach pie thing all over again. I open the door and the only thing I say is, "I'm going in before the place closes."

I go on in, not waiting on her, and the guy behind the counter says, "Help you?"

"I'm here to pick up my dog."

"What's the name?"

"Boone."

"I'll call and make sure Boone is ready to go."

For a second I don't understand, and then I get it. "No, my dog's name is Frankie. I'm Boone."

He's got the phone to his ear already, but he turns to me and grins a little. "Frankie. Right."

In about half a minute the door to the back of the place opens up and Frankie comes out. The main vet, the old man, has a tight hold on her, but he almost loses control of her when she sees me.

I'm down on my knees and Frankie is all over me and everything is good. I wipe my face and look up and the vet is smiling. I look around and so is everybody else. Nancy is standing at the front door and she's got tears in her eyes.

"When you two get finished saying hello I need to go over some stuff with you," the vet says. He's close enough now that the leash is slack, and he looks around and sees Nancy. "Will you hold onto this, young lady? I need to go get some paperwork."

She takes the leash and Frankie notices the movement and sees Nancy. She goes straight to her, then back to me, and does that three or four times and then Nancy steps over close to me and all at once the three of us are on the floor hugging and Frankie's making those little noises that she makes when she's really happy.

The vet shows me what they did and tells me what to watch for and gives me some kind of medicine that he says Frankie needs twice a day after the bandages come off. I'm supposed to change them tomorrow or, if everything looks good, I can leave them off and start with this tube of stuff. He wants to see her in a few days.

It takes the two hundred plus most of what I already had in my wallet, but I don't even mind.

"Thanks," I say.

He says, "This is the best part of the job, seeing you and Frankie together. She's going to be fine, Boone. Just be careful where you let her run."

Out in the parking lot I put Frankie in the back and start to get in the front seat and Nancy says, "I bet if we put Frankie back there and we're both up here it won't last to the end of the parking lot. She'll be over the seat and trying to get in both our laps. You ought to ride back there and hang on to her."

I know she's right, so I close the door and open the back door, climb in, and put my arms around Frankie.

"You want to close your door, sweetie?"

I look up and Nancy's laughing and pointing to the open back door.

On the way from the parking lot down to my place I notice Frankie's limp. It's not bad but she's definitely favoring that leg. She's not trying to pull away from me either, just heading down the hill to the house. Nancy's right beside me, not talking, just squeezing my hand every once in a while.

Frankie goes straight to the water bowl and drinks it almost dry, then heads for her blanket and lies down.

I start to say something to Nancy and there's a knock on the door. When I open it, Mark is standing there. "I thought I saw you come into the parking lot. How's Frankie?" He steps inside and sees Nancy. "Oh, hi, Nancy, were you the driver?"

"Boone wouldn't have been able to drive, Mark, Frankie was all over him."

He laughs. "I'd bet it was mutual." He turns to me. "How is she doing?"

I nod and point to Frankie, who's barely awake. She raises her head and looks at Mark, then puts it back down again.

"Just glad to be home, I guess," I say.

Mark goes over to Frankie and squats down next to her. "You okay, girl?"

She starts to get up and Mark puts his hand on her back, up close to her head. "You need your rest, Frankie. Don't get up on my account."

He gives her a quick scratch behind the ears and straightens up.

"She looks a lot better, I'll bet."

"Yeah, the vet says she's going to be fine."

"Well, I just wanted to check. I'll let Betty know you're back with Frankie and tell her what the vet said."

He heads out the door and I plop down on the couch. All of a sudden I'm just worn out.

Nancy sits down beside me. She doesn't say anything, and I guess I must have really not slept at all last night, because the next thing I remember is Frankie nudging me to wake up and let her out. She's pushing on my right leg and I start to move and realize that my left arm's caught under something. I turn my head and my chin grazes the top of Nancy's head. My arm is down next to my body and she is snuggled up next to me.

It's still light outside, so I can't have been asleep all that long. Frankie is pushing against me and I'm trying not to move, because this right here is better than anything that's happened to me in quite a while. Nancy moves a little and her hand drops from my chest into my lap.

I jump a little, just enough to wake her up. I can't help it, it surprises me, but if I could do it all again, I'd have stayed still as a mouse with a hawk up in the sky. She moves her head off my shoulder and then I guess she realizes where her hand is. She jerks it back and scoots away from me.

"Sorry, sorry," she's talking so low I can barely hear her. Frankie is heading toward the door; she's glad somebody finally is up and ready to take her outside.

"Me too," I say. "I mean, I'm sorry I woke you up."

She gives me a quick look and I swear there's a smile on her lips. Then she's trying to be real serious and says, "Listen, Boone, I told Mom I'd be home for supper and I'm already late." She waves her cell phone at me. "Look at the time. I can't believe she hasn't called me already. I've got to go right now, but I'm sure glad Frankie's okay. You're okay, right, girl?" She leans down and rubs Frankie on her head and then straightens up. "Walk me to the car?"

"Sure. Let me get Frankie's leash and I'll take her with us. She needs to go out anyway."

On the way to the parking lot I try to keep my arm around Nancy's waist, but Frankie keeps nosing in between us, and by the time we get to her car, we're both laughing.

"You call me soon, okay?" she says. "When do you go back to the vet?"

"Not for a few days," I say.

"Okay, well, call me before that."

"I will." I grin at her. "You know that's the first time I ever slept with a girl."

She's as red as a beet. "Boone Hammond, don't you dare tell anybody that!" She pushes me away and says, "Go on now, I've got to get home."

I try to call her the next day, but she doesn't answer, and I don't like to leave messages. It feels weird talking to a machine like that.

Saturday about ten in the morning somebody wakes me up banging on the door. Frankie is up and wagging her tail, so I open the door and Tiny is standing there.

"Hey, man, how's it going?" Then I get a look at his face.

"What's wrong?"

"You still got that shine recipe?"

"Yeah, it's in the kitchen, in the drawer. Why?"

"Because that's all you've got left, Boone. That and whatever shine we haven't drunk up yet."

"What the hell are you talking about?"

I'm trying to keep from shouting and not doing such a great job, so I reach out and grab his arm and pull him inside. I slam the door and Frankie jumps back.

Tiny is already on the couch, and he's filthy. His jeans are torn and dirty and I can smell smoke coming off him like he's been camping out on one of the lake islands and spent all night sitting by the fire.

"You got any water, man?"

"In the kitchen. You'll have to get it out of the sink. You going to tell me what happened? You look like shit."

He goes into the kitchen and drinks three glasses of water standing right there at the sink before he comes back in and plops down on the couch again.

"It didn't start at the still, I'm pretty sure about that."

"What didn't start?"

"The brush fire. You know nobody's done anything with that land next to ours for who knows how long. Some of it you can't hardly hack your way through. They're trying to figure out how it started, but me and the rest of my family have been up there all night, trying to keep it from spreading to our land. The fire burned away that tarp I had on all our stuff and as soon as the firefighters saw the setup they called the sheriff. It's all burnt up, all the supplies, and the law's got the coil and the other stuff. They asked me about it and I said I hardly ever come up to that part of the property, and anyway that's not our land up there, and I'm pretty sure they believed me. Anyway, it's gone. You better drink what you've got left real slow, man. There isn't going to be any more. Not from that still, anyway."

I can't think what to say.

"What the hell happened to Frankie?" He's looking at her back leg, and I realize I haven't talked to him for the last few days.

"Tell you later. It's all gone?"

He nods.

I just stand there. Gamaliel and my daddy had that still for years and nothing happened to it. I take over and it's already gone. Maybe Daddy was right about me. Maybe I'm a useless piece of shit after all.

Tiny's back at the sink. He's drinking slower now, and sets his glass down after only filling it up the one time.

I start to say, so what do we do now? and don't because there's nothing to do.

Chapter Twenty-One

"I need a drink," I finally say, looking at the floor.

Tiny starts laughing and pretty soon he's doubled over on the couch. He finally gets his breath and sits up.

"Hell, yeah, let's have one. Or two."

I make two the way Gamaliel would want me to and bring them back into the little living room. Tiny stands up and takes one of the glasses from me and raises it up. "To the old man."

I raise mine up too, but I don't say anything because I don't want to start crying in front of Tiny.

He takes his all in one drink and shakes his head, hard. "Damnation, I forgot how he liked his. I better sit back down." And he does. I take the glass from him and put it on the floor next to the corner of the couch and sit down beside him. I take a little longer with mine but pretty soon we're both just sitting there staring at the floor. Nobody says anything for a while and then Tiny says, "I believe one's going to be enough for me."

He stands up and says, "I got to go check for hot spots. If that fire gets into our buildings they'd be gone in no time flat."

"Need some help?"

"Every bit we can get. It's a big damn mess up there. You sure you don't need to stay here with Frankie?"

As soon as he says that I remember that Frankie can't go with us, and I'm about to tell him to go on, that I'd better stay here. Feels like I need to go up there and help, though. Tiny would do it for me in a heartbeat, I know that.

"I'll get Mark to watch her. Or Betty."

He nods and heads for the door. "I'll see you up there. I got to get going."

After he's gone I sit and stare at Frankie for a long time, thinking about Daddy. One of the worst beatings I ever got, maybe the worst, was when he came up on me and Curt out in the field where he is now. We weren't more than ten or so and Curt had brought a box of those big kitchen matches and we were flicking them at each other. We'd set the head of the match on the side of the box and press down hard on the other end with our finger and flip at it with our other hand, middle finger behind the thumb and then pow, as hard as we could, If we hit it just right it would light and fly toward the other guy. Curt was better than me but I was starting to get the hang of it when Daddy showed up.

Looking back I know he was real scared, but all he showed us was mad. Curt got out of there in a hurry and I got the shit beat out of me. He sent me back to the house and when I turned and looked back at him he was stomping all over the place where me and Curt had been. I didn't know why he cared so much about it, it wasn't even his house or barn or anything.

I finally snap out of it and stand up. "C'mon, Frankie, let's go see Mark," I say.

When I get to Tiny's place there are half a dozen trucks parked all over the yard and Mrs. Thompson is walking toward the house from the field. She looks like hell, like she fell off her four by four and it dragged her a ways.

"Everybody's still up there, Boone," she points toward where the still used to be. "I think they're making progress but I sure am glad to see you. It's pretty damn awful, worst I've seen since I was a little girl."

I start to ask about that but she's already inside the house. There's nobody else around, so I head out through the back yard and into the field.

Everything looks the same until I top that first hill. The land drops down a little and then back up toward the wood line, and I can hear men's voices and see people moving around, in and out of the trees.

There are foot trails through the grass where people have been back and forth from the Thompson place up to the woods, and I follow one of them down and back up toward where the still used to be. A couple of guys look in my direction and then right back down to the ground, moving their heads back and forth. I can't see what they're looking at from where I am.

Three of them are leaning up against that big rock that Tiny and I used as a landmark, drinking from a gallon milk jug they are passing back and forth. One of them splashes a little water from it on his face and I hear another one say, "Damn, Mike, if you're going to pour it out just hand it on over. I'm dry as a bone."

I come up to them and they nod at me, but don't offer me a drink. They can tell by how clean I am that I just got here. I stand there for a minute and finally say, "Tiny around anywhere?"

Mike points toward a bunch of guys about thirty feet into the woods. "Think he's over there." I nod and head that way.

When I get close Tiny looks over his shoulder and waves me into the group. One of the others looks at me and says, "Where's your gloves?"

I just stand there.

"You planning to do this bare-handed? That'll last about a half a minute," the same guy says, and it sounds just like all those times I been made fun all my life and I'm about ready to shove his gloves right up his ass and head on back to the truck when Tiny says, "You know those gloves you left here when you helped me clean out that shed? I let Gary over there have them but I've got another pair you can use," and he tosses me a pair of gloves that smell like smoke already.

I'm really dragging by the time somebody comes around with a jug of water. This is a lot harder work than I've done in a while and pretty damn depressing work on top of that. Somebody working close to me said it was early in the year for this kind of fire, that it usually happens in the fall, but that these woods were so grown up that it wouldn't take much.

"You know they found a still right over there," he says, pointing back to the rock. "I bet some damn fool was up here making shine and went off and left the fire going, and now look what we've got. Damn fools," he says again, pulling a black branch aside to look under it for anything still burning.

I almost tell him that we weren't cooking any mash right now so it couldn't have been us and catch myself just in time.

Surely Tiny wasn't up here working without me.

The guy with the water is gone, making the rounds to everybody else, so I get back to work. The group I'm in, four of us altogether, are working around the side of the hill, just across the fence from the Thompson's land. There are two guys out ahead of me, and the one in front is about thirty yards away when he stops in his tracks and says, "Oh, shit, oh, shit! Somebody call the sheriff, quick!"

He looks back and catches my eye. "Move your ass, kid! I said get somebody over here! It looks like we got a dead guy at the base of that big tree over there!"

It's like I can't move for a second, and then I turn and start back toward the rock, looking for Tiny or Mrs. Thompson. I don't know anybody else up here. By that time the other guy that used to be ahead of me is past me and moving fast, shouting for somebody named Bowden. I don't have any idea who that is.

I start after him, trying to keep up. There's so many branches and vines, all grey and black and no leaves, that I keep tripping and a couple of times I almost fall on my face. I don't get very far before I see him coming back with a big guy, bigger than Tiny even. I have to jump sideways to get out of their way.

After they go by I turn around and follow behind, and pretty much everybody on the hill is right behind me. We get close to the tree, about twenty feet, and the big guy and three others are standing there in a line with their arms stretched out wide.

"Keep back, y'all," one of them is saying, over and over.

We're all crowded together in sort of a line facing the three guys guarding the tree. I can see what used to be a person, a man I guess, sitting on the ground leaned against the trunk of the tree. His hand is flopped down on the ground beside him and I can see something right next to it.

It's a meth pipe.

I can't see his other hand, but I bet there's a lighter in it.

"Guess it wasn't the still after all," the guy next to me says, and I look over at him. It's the same man I was next to before all this started. He doesn't look too good.

He glances as me and then at the tree, and takes a step back. "Never seen anything like that before," he says, mostly to himself, and then turns around and almost runs away from the group.

He's not the only one. About half the men are going back across the hill, away from the tree, and two or three of them are in the Thompson's field already, heading toward the house.

"Wonder who that is," the man on the other side of me says. "Might be hard to figure out. He's burnt up pretty good."

I'm wondering if it's the same pipe I saw at the abandoned house over on the highway. That's pretty far from here, I think, but I'm not sure about going cross country. Still seems like a long ways. It sort of looks like the same pipe, but I know that doesn't mean anything. There's probably a dozen just like it within a few miles of here.

I look away from the dead guy and try to figure out where that house might be, and when I step out of the woods I see that I'm pretty far away from the Thompson house already. Their field goes on around the side of the hill; I can see the fence at the edge of it and more woods past the fence. I start walking that way and when I get close to the fence and see a creek running through the woods about twenty yards in I know exactly where I am.

Turning away from the fence, I take a half a dozen steps down the hill and even though the trees on the lower side of the field aren't burnt I can see through them enough to see a little of the back of Gamaliel's house. Over to the left, too far away for me to see, is the house I used to live in and the field where Daddy is buried.

There's a noise behind me and I turn around and see Tiny coming toward me.

"Did you see the dead guy?"

I nod.

Tiny shakes his head. "Almost lost whatever was still in my stomach." He gives me a look. "Didn't bother you?"

I start to say I've seen lots worse but I can't. I can't ever tell anybody about Daddy.

"I wasn't that close."

"Neither was I, and I still almost threw up on the guy next to me." He laughs that short laugh. "It was Joe Meechum. That would've been bad."

"I don't know who that is."

"He owns Mountain Laurel Bank, lives two hills over." Tiny points back away from the creek toward his house. "He wears a suit all the time and acts like he's a big shot, which I guess he is, but mostly he's okay. He did come to help with the hot spots." He laughs again. "Don't want to throw up on a guy I might have to ask for a loan someday."

"I guess not."

Tiny nods toward his place. "Here comes the ambulance. Wonder how close they'll be able to get. Couple of ditches in this field. I'd better go warn them, don't want them to break an axle." He takes off, walking fast.

Chapter Twenty-Two

We work on into the night. The hot spots are a lot easier to see after the sun goes down. There's only a few, glowing underneath the ash and branches, and we wet them or stomp them out.

About half the guys went home before sunset, so it's a small group, but we're in pretty good shape, I think. I see Tiny and go over to him.

"What do you think?"

He looks as tired as I've ever seen him, but he's nodding his head. "Good. I think we're good. Damn, this wore me out, Boone. You been home to check on Frankie yet?"

I shake my head.

He reaches in his pocket and hands me his phone. "Why don't you give Mark or Betty or whoever a call? Tell them we're getting close to finishing up here."

I walk off and make the call.

"Hello?" It's a woman.

"Uh, is Mark there?" I say.

"There's no Mark here," she says. She sounds a little mad.

"Oh, sorry, I was trying—"

"I know where you were trying for. Check your number. It's 63, not 36. I get these calls all the time."

I start to say thanks, but she's already hung up on me. I'm surprised I got that close to the number, since I hardly ever call. I try again and get it right this time, and they connect me to Mark.

"Hey, Mark, it's Boone. Is Frankie okay?"

"She's fine, Boone. You've been gone a while. Everything all right up there?"

"Yeah, we're about to finish up. You hear about the dead guy?"

"What are you talking about, Boone? What dead guy?"

I tell him about the woods, and the still, and how we were working around the side of the hill and the lead guy found somebody sitting under a big tree.

"Looked to me like he had a meth pipe," I say.

Mark doesn't say anything.

"Listen, I got to go, I'm on Tiny's phone. Take care of Frankie and I'll be back pretty soon."

I hand the phone back to Tiny and he starts to leave, then turns back. "You know it wasn't us started this, right?"

I nod.

"I figure it was that guy they found, probably had a heart attack or something and when he dropped all his stuff it set it off."

I nod again. Ever since I saw that guy I've been relieved. Gamaliel was always real careful about fire and he got all over my ass if I wasn't, so I didn't think it was anything we did. Still feels good to hear Tiny say that, especially since it's his farm that just about went up.

"Ready to get back to it?"

"Yeah. What's next?"

"I want to walk our fence all the way across the burn area now that it's dark. They're not calling for rain for another day or so, and I don't want to miss anything. I've got a flashlight but anything still glowing will be a lot easier to see in the dark. You okay with walking it without lights?"

"I'm good. Listen, where's Eunuch?"

Tiny grins. "You know that building you helped me clean out? He's in there, I put him up before we all came up here. He's driving Mom crazy, I'd say."

It takes about an hour to walk the fence line. Tiny goes real slow, stopping about every three steps to look up into the woods. "What I wish I'd done," he says one time we're both staring at all that blackness, "is plow a firebreak right along here. I might do that tomorrow morning. If Lyle was here, he would've thought of it right away and we wouldn't have to worry about anything but wind."

I haven't heard that name in a while. Last time I saw Tiny's older brother was way back when the Thompsons used to have those bonfires. He was a couple of years ahead of Tiny and when I would see him he was usually heading off into the woods with one of the girls.

"Where is he anyway?"

Tiny doesn't answer for a minute and then says, "Don't tell anybody, all right?"

"Okay."

"He got himself into some trouble over in Little Rock. He's about halfway through an eleven twenty-nine."

I don't know just what that is, so I don't say anything.

Tiny goes on, "He got in a bar fight, the damn fool. Second time in the same bar, and this time they called the law. Mom doesn't want to talk about it, but I think he gave the police some trouble when they came to break it up, and the judge had a stick up his ass about something or other and gave him just shy of a year. Anyway, don't spread that around. Mom doesn't want anybody around here to know about it."

"He got a year in jail for getting in a fight?"

"Well, I think he'd had a couple of run-ins with the police already. Used a couple of stop signs for target practice, shit like that. So this time, you know, I guess they were just tired of fooling with him."

He can't see me smiling in the dark, but I can't help but think about all those times I thought the Thompsons were just about perfect. A few years ago Tiny's dad got a license to be a long-haul trucker, he's gone about all the time, so his mom pretty much runs things, and she doesn't put up with any shit of any kind. I'll bet it's killing her to have her boy in jail.

"So how far away is Little Rock?"

"About five, maybe six hundred miles. We don't go over there to see him. I think Dad was driving right through there once, didn't even slow down."

"Damn."

"Remember, keep this to yourself, Boone. It's nobody's business."

"Sure. So are you doing this firebreak tomorrow?"

"Yeah. It won't take long at all, and I'm probably doing it for no good reason, but I'll feel better. Who do you think that was up in the woods?"

I shrug. "I don't know any meth users, at least there's nobody that I can think of that does that shit. It's supposed to be really bad."

He shakes his head. "Me neither. Hope it's nobody we know."

Chapter Twenty-Three

By the time I get home it's really late, but I go by Mark's office anyway. His light is off, but the door is open just a crack. When I get close, I hear Frankie get up and start moving around, so I push the door open.

She's on her leash, tied to one leg of Mark's desk. Mark is sitting in his chair, rubbing his eyes and trying to wake up.

"What time is it?"

Then he looks at the clock on his desk and says, "Never mind. It's one in the morning, Boone. You just now getting in?"

"Yeah, it was a long day." I sit down in one of the chairs and Frankie comes over, sniffing at my jeans. I'm covered in soot, even though I tried to brush off before I even got in my truck. Mark frowns.

"You smell like you were rolling in ashes, Boone. So how bad was it?"

"Not too bad, the fire's out, pretty much, and it's supposed to rain tomorrow or the next day. We just looked for hot spots and there weren't too many of those."

"Well, you look awful. I want to hear about this dead man you all found, but what you need right now is a hot shower and some clean clothes, and what I need is a few hours of sleep in my own bed. I'm going to get out of here. If you're okay, that is." He looks at me and I nod.

"Yeah, I'm headed down to the house. Thanks for taking care of Frankie."

"She's no trouble, Boone, she's a really good dog. But you already knew that."

I don't wake up until after ten and Frankie is nosing at me to either feed her or take her out or both. I get my hands under me and start to push up off the bed and flop right back down. Every muscle I've got is hurting. Yesterday was long and hard; that's not what I told Mark when I got in, and while it was going on it didn't seem that bad. Now anything I move lights up like it's on fire. The most I can do is roll over on my back and lie there waiting for my muscles to stop aching.

There never was that much to do around the house when Daddy was around, he was always off working for somebody else and when he got home he was usually so pissed off he'd just sit and drink or yell at one or the other of us. Besides, it wasn't his place, not really, and if he ever did decide to do something and got me helping him, it wouldn't be five minutes before he was yelling at me or calling me a baby or a pussy or something. So I never did much there, never got in the habit of doing any real work.

One thing about Daddy, though, he could work most men his age into the ground when he took a mind to. All those years out in the fields working in hay or tobacco or tomatoes or whatever work was around toughened him up. The few times I crossed him I paid for it; he handled me like I was nothing, and that made him mad at me all over again because I couldn't stand up against him. Frankie died before he got old enough to have to go against Daddy; wonder how that would have gone.

I'm still there on the bed and Frankie trots off toward the front door. I hear it open and close and then Nancy says, "Oh!" and I look up and she's standing in the hallway looking in at me. It takes me a second to remember that last night after I took that shower I just fell onto the bed, didn't even get under the covers.

"I'll be out there in a minute," I say. "I got to get some clothes on." I stare at the ceiling and think about how bad it's going to hurt to try to sit up.

"You ought to lock your front door. Wouldn't want your housekeeper barging in and seeing you like that," she says.

"Even if she opened the door, as soon as she saw Frankie she'd be gone," I say, trying to decide whether or not to cover myself up. "She's afraid of dogs." I reach for the edge of the blanket.

"You know," she says. "I've never seen you this way before. Actually," she's barely whispering now, "I've never seen anybody this way before."

I'm embarrassed and excited all at the same time, and I don't know what to do.

She's still whispering. "It scares me to death, thinking what I'm thinking right now." Her voice gets louder. "Maybe you ought to get some clothes on, sweetie. I'm going to go sit on the couch."

I manage to sit up, and I put on the only clean blue jeans I've got. When I get out into the living room Nancy is sitting next to Frankie and has a glass half full in her hand. She holds it up. "Water," she says. "If I had anything stronger I'm afraid I'd drag you right back into the bedroom."

"It's just as well you didn't have any shine," I say. "There's only so much left."

I go in and start to fix an S&S for myself and decide to have water instead. I carry it back to the couch and sit down next to Nancy. She reaches over and rubs my chest and says, "You know, I've seen pictures and all that, but it's not the same." Her hand slides down a little and then she jerks it away.

I feel like I'm going crazy.

"I just came over to see how Frankie was getting along," she continues, "and I sure didn't mean to walk in on you like that."

"It's okay," I shrug my shoulders. "I wish I could move a little better, you know? You must be burning up with all those clothes on." I try to grin, and I reach my hand out toward her and have to drop it; it hurts to hold it out away from me.

"What's wrong?" She starts to put her hand on my arm and then stops. "You hurt your arm?"

"You didn't hear about the fire up at Tiny's?"

She shakes her head. "No, but I thought I smelled smoke when I opened your door. What fire? When? Is Tiny okay?"

"He's fine. It's not bad, I just ache all over. Didn't get in until up in the morning. Frankie hasn't even been out yet today, bet she's going to pee all over the house if I don't get her outside."

"Well, let's take her out. You can tell me all about what happened. Want me to hold her leash?"

I don't want Frankie jerking me all over the place right now. I'm sore enough as it is.

"Sure. Frankie, you want to go out?"

We get outside, Nancy holding Frankie, and I start telling her about the fire. She stops me when I say the still is gone and says, "Did you and Tiny start this fire? Oh, sweetie, that'd be awful!"

I shake my head. "I haven't been up there in a few weeks. We were thinking about starting a new batch, but we hadn't done anything yet."

"Thank goodness."

"I think it was the dead guy that started the fire," I say, my eyes on the ground in front of me.

She doesn't say anything and I look over after a few more steps and she's not there. She and Frankie are a few steps back and she's standing there with her mouth wide open.

I turn around and head back to them. The soreness is working out of my muscles and I'm starting to feel okay. And hungry. I'm really hungry.

"Listen," I say, pointing at Frankie. She's out at the end of the leash squatting in the grass. "Let's go back to the house or go out somewhere. I'm about to starve."

"What dead guy? Boone, what in the hell are you talking about? Did somebody burn up in the fire? Who was it? Were you the one that found him?"

"We don't know who it is. Somebody else found him, leaning against a tree. I think he was smoking meth and had a heart attack or something."

Nancy looks like she's about to cry. "What a terrible way to die, Boone, that's so sad."

I don't say anything.

"I mean," she goes on, "I've never seen a dead person before, except at funerals."

She hesitates like she wants me to say something, but I'm not going to. Right now I'm seeing Daddy, and I can't say anything about that to anybody.

"Sweetie, are you all right? You're a thousand miles away."

I nod and then say, "Yeah. Can we go get some food? I'm really hungry."

We head back to the house and get there about the same time as Mark. He's stepping up to the door when he sees us. "Hello, Nancy! Good to see you again! Taking Boone out for a walk?"

She looks at him for a second and then laughs. "Yeah, I forgot to put him on a leash, but he stayed pretty close."

All I can think about is how hungry I am. And Daddy. Can't stop thinking about him.

Mark looks at me. "You okay, Boone? Get any sleep?"

"Yeah, I was just waking up when Nancy came in — I mean, when she got here."

Mark raises his eyebrows but doesn't say anything, and I don't say anything else.

Finally he says, "Tell me about finding this person in the fire. That must have been terrible. Oh," he stops and looks at Nancy, "I didn't think. Has Boone told you about last night?"

She nods. "Not much, but some. He—"

I'm afraid she's about to slip up and tell him about the still. "I didn't tell her much about the dead guy because I don't know much. He was just there, you know?"

"I talked to the police right after you called me last night, Boone. They didn't know who he was and they told me it might be really hard to find out. He was badly burned. They were waiting for the coroner to finish with him."

"I know that, Mark. I saw him." I turn to Nancy. "You want to go get something to eat? I'm going to put Frankie in the house and get out of here."

"Sure, sweetie," she says, looking sideways at Mark. "Want me to drive?"

"I don't much care who drives, long as we go. There's nothing much in the fridge here, so let's go. Somewhere close."

I start toward the parking lot and then remember. I go back to Nancy and get Frankie's leash. "Let me get her some food and I'll be right out."

"Don't forget to put a shirt on," she calls after me.

"Okay!" Frankie jumps a little and looks up at me. She goes in ahead of me and I check her food and water, take off the leash, and squat down beside her.

"I wasn't yelling at you, girl," I say, stroking her head and trying to calm down. "I'll be back in a little bit."

She licks my face and then goes over to her blanket.

I stand back up and look around the room, but all I can see is that dead guy, or Daddy. They jump in and out of my head and there's no room for anything else. I go into the kitchen and grab a glass, and I'm about to pour a strong one when the glass slips out of my hand and crashes to the floor.

I stand there shaking, looking at the broken glass. After a minute I get down and start picking it up, and I don't hear the door open.

Then Nancy is down on her hands and knees beside me, getting the little pieces that I'm missing. She doesn't say a word, doesn't even look at me. She's making sure she gets every little bit of glass.

Chapter Twenty-Four

We're almost to the closest place to eat before either one of us says anything.

Nancy is the first one to talk.

"So what are you hungry for? This place has burgers and stuff like that, but if you want pizza there's a lot better place about another mile down this way."

I don't answer right away and she says it again. We've already passed the first place.

"What do you want to eat, Boone? There's three or four places we can go."

"I don't care. Somewhere close. Up there." I point to a place up on the right.

"Sounds good. They've got those little sliders I like and you can get, you know, whatever. My treat."

I look over at her and then back to the road. "Thanks."

She gets a little square chicken sandwich and I get a burger and fries. She gets a paper cup of ketchup and I look at it and then go back for two more.

She's looking at me when I come back to the table and I put them down and say, "I like ketchup."

Nancy nods and picks up her chicken sandwich, takes a bite.

When she puts it down she reaches for a fry and then stops and looks up at me.

I shrug. "Take as many as you want."

"You sure?"

I don't say anything and after a second she picks one of the little ones and dips it in the ketchup.

The burger is good with a little extra ketchup, and I finish it pretty quick. Nancy eats about half my fries, but I don't mind. It's her money.

"You okay?"

I look over at her and she's staring at me. I look around and there's only about three or four more people in the restaurant and they're all busy eating and looking at some game on the TV.

"Yeah. I guess that dead guy, well, I guess he bothered me more than I thought."

"I just can't imagine. I mean, it must've been awful."

"Tiny said he almost threw up all over the bank president."

She laughs out loud and then stops herself. "I'm sorry. That's not funny. I mean, somebody died."

"It's kind of funny." I try to smile at her. The food's helping a lot; I must have been really hungry.

"I never met Mr. Meechum, but I've seen him in the bank and at church. He's always dressed up," she stops for a second and starts smiling, "so, yeah, it is kind of funny. He wasn't in his suit, was he?"

I shake my head.

"You want some dessert or something?"

She's got a menu in her hand and I say, "What kind of stuff do they have?"

"Well," she says, "they've got three or four different kinds of pie and something called a volcano that has cake and ice cream and, like, a ton of chocolate sauce poured all over it. It's huge, look at it," and she hands me the menu. She points to the top corner and I say, "I've never had anything like that before."

"So you want to split it?"

She's looking at me like I'm supposed to say yes, so I say, "Sure. Why not?"

"Okay," She waves her hand and a girl about her age comes over. "Hey, Sandy, we're going for the volcano."

Sandy grins. "It's a monster. You want two spoons, right? One for you and one for . . . ."

"Oh, sorry," Nancy says. "This is Boone. He promised to help me eat it."

200

"Hi, Boone. You're going to love it, I guarantee it."
She heads off and Nancy says, "She was a year ahead
of me in school. I heard she was going into the Navy,
maybe next month."

"What's the big deal with the Navy? Somebody's
trying to get Tiny to sign up, too."

"Really? Maybe that same recruiter got to him.
She's been after Sandy for a month or more."

Sandy comes back over with a big bowl and two
spoons. She reaches in her apron and pulls out a
stack of napkins. She sets them down beside the
volcano. "You'll need every one of them. You two
enjoy; be careful, that fudge sauce is still pretty hot."

The volcano has a big slab of chocolate cake in the
bowl and four scoops of vanilla ice cream piled on top
of it. Looks like about a quart of chocolate sauce
poured over the ice cream and running down the
sides and into the bowl. Damned if it doesn't look
kind of like a volcano, except for the glob of whipped
cream on the very top. Nancy picks up her spoon.

"You can sit there and stare at it if you want to,
Boone. I'm not waiting."

She takes a spoonful of ice cream and runs it
through the sauce. She puts it in her mouth and
leans back on her chair. "Oh my God, that's good!
Boone, sweetie, you have to get started on this or I'll
eat it all. Here," and she hands me my spoon. "Get
going. You're already behind."

By the time we finish it there's only one napkin left and I feel like I'm going to bust. I look across at Nancy. "That might be the best thing I've ever put in my mouth."

"Told you." She runs her spoon around the inside of the bowl and lifts it out. It's about half full of chocolate sauce and a few crumbs of cake. The ice cream is long gone. "Want the last bite?"

"You go ahead. I don't think I can even stand up as it is."

She licks the spoon clean and tosses it into the bowl and says, "Let's get out of here,"

On the way back to my place we don't talk; I look over at Nancy now and then and she's got a smile on her face the whole time. She pulls into a parking spot and turns toward me and leans over the console and I think she's getting ready to kiss me. Instead she pokes me in the gut and I think I'm about to throw up all over her car.

She's laughing so hard she can't hardly say anything, but finally says, "That's the other reason they call it the volcano. Don't you dare erupt all over my car, Boone Hammond."

When we get back to the house I fall back on the couch and Nancy sits down next to me. I look at her.

"If I wouldn't have to worry about it getting all over me I'd give you a poke like you gave me up in the car."

She grins. "I think you're too late, sweetie, I'm more or less settled down."

"Let's see." I start to reach out my hand and she grabs it real quick. "Let's not," she says.

"That's okay," I say, and I let my hand fall back on the couch. "I'd better get back up to Tiny's anyway."

"I thought you said it wasn't bad."

"I don't think it is, but Tiny said something about plowing a fire break and checking one more time, and I just thought I'd go on up there and see if he needed anything."

"Well, I know he'd appreciate it," she says. "Maybe I shouldn't have made you split that volcano with me."

"Don't worry about it," I say. "I'll be all right once I get off this couch."

It takes me a couple of times to get up, mostly because of the volcano. The soreness is about gone, and when I get up I stretch my arms out and they barely hurt.

"I think I'm good," I tell her. "I appreciate the lunch; that was pretty good."

"You going to take Frankie with you?"

I shake my head. "I think I'll stop by Mark's office and see if he can watch her. Or maybe Betty. Mark had her until way late last night. Frankie's good about finding a spot in his office and just laying down, and I don't think I'll be gone as long this time.

He might tell me to come on back as soon as I get up there."

"Want me to stay here and keep an eye on her?"

I look down at her and then over at Frankie. "What do you think, girl? You want to hang out with Nancy for a while?"

Nancy says, "You get on out of here, Boone. I've got Frankie. I'll call Mom and tell her I'm going to be a little late getting home, in case Tiny needs you for longer than you think."

When I get up to the Thompson place there's only a couple of cars in the yard and Mrs. Thompson is there in the back looking up the hill.

"Hi, Boone. Tiny says you stayed up here late last night. I sure thank you for that."

"It's nothing, Mrs. Thompson, he'd do it for me. Is he up there?"

She nods. "There's not much to do. Looks like everything's out and they're calling for rain. He probably doesn't even need to plow that fire break, but he insisted. Want me to tell him you stopped by?"

"I was thinking I'd go up and see if he needed anything."

She shakes her head. "There's no need. He's been up there for a little bit already, and you'd probably meet him coming back on the tractor. You're welcome to stay, though, have a glass of ice tea, and wait on him."

"Thanks, but I'd better not have any tea. Nancy made me split a volcano with her after lunch, and I'm about to bust."

"I"m surprised you can walk, Boone. I was in that restaurant a week or two ago and somebody tried to eat one by himself. He stopped before he was half done, and he was a big boy. Not as big as Phillip, you understand, but still."

"You're sure he doesn't need anything?"

She nods. "I'm sure. He'd appreciate that you came by, Boone, and I'll let him know."

I turn around and start back toward the truck. She says, "You know they figured out who that was up there in the woods?"

That stops me cold. "That was fast. How'd they do that?"

I can hear her coming toward me and in a second she's right next to me. "They found his wallet when they moved the body. He was sitting on it, you know, so the fire didn't get to it as bad."

"Somebody from around here?"

She's watching me close when she says, "Yes, it was. Well, not really, but he had family here."

I'm looking at my feet, trying to think who it might be, and then I think I know what she's going to say next. I remember looking around after we found him and realizing where I was.

"How well did you know Gamaliel's family, Boone?"

I shrug. "Not so much, I guess. A little."

"Did you know his son-in-law Jerry?"

I nod. "Met him a few times."

She doesn't say anything and I finally look at her and say, "Was it him?"

She nods. "When I told Tiny I thought I was going to have to grab hold of him to keep him from falling over. He said he met Jerry down at Gamaliel's house once when you were staying there. Said he was really drunk and it was early in the day, not even suppertime yet."

I'm just standing there.

She's still talking. "Somebody said he gave up drinking, but maybe he just moved on to something a lot worse."

"Maybe so."

"I feel so bad for Gamaliel's daughter, what was her name?"

"Carrie," I say. "Her name is Carrie."

"Right. I feel so bad for her."

"Listen, Mrs. Thompson, I better get on back home, if you're sure Tiny doesn't need me. You tell him I stopped by, okay?"

"I'll do that, Boone. Thanks again for helping us out last night." She gives me a look. "You sure you're okay?"

"Fine, Mrs. Thompson. Listen, I better go."

All the way back home I'm thinking about Jerry.

Nancy is surprised to see me back so quick. "I didn't think we'd see you for hours. Frankie and I were just getting ready for another walk. You want to go with us?"

I shake my head and sit down on the couch. "Go on ahead. I'll just wait here."

"What's wrong, sweetie?" Nancy comes over and sits down beside me. She puts her hand on my leg and I don't even look at it or at her. She calls Frankie over.

"Listen, Frankie, we're going to stay in for a minute or two, okay?"

She turns back to me. "Okay, Boone, what happened up at Tiny's? Is he okay?"

I nod.

"Then what is it?"

I raise my head up to look at her. "They figured out who the dead guy was."

Chapter Twenty-Five

"Oh, God, Boone, is it somebody you knew?"

I nod. "You knew him, too, darlin'." I have to stop for a second. "It was Jerry."

Nancy puts both hands up on her cheeks. "Oh, Boone. Oh, poor Carrie. Does she know yet? Of course she knows, she'd have to know if Tiny knows. Did Tiny tell you who it was? When did he find out?"

She finally stops talking and just sits there for a minute.

I stand up. "I got to go tell Mark about Jerry. And Betty. She knows Carrie, both of them do."

"I'll go up there with you," Nancy says, and stands up too. She reaches for her phone. "I'll call Mom and let her know I'm going to be here for a while. No, wait. I already did that. She needs to know about this, though. I need to call her."

"Go ahead."

After she calls her mom we start to leave and I go back to the kitchen to make sure Frankie has enough water. She's got plenty, and we leave her in the house and walk up to the main building.

Mark is just opening his office door when we come in the side entrance.

"Hello, Nancy," he says. "Hi, Boone. Did you get enough sleep? I didn't know whether I'd see you again today or not."

After a second he says, "What's wrong?" and I realize I'm just standing there staring at him. I feel Nancy grab my hand and she says, "Can we get out of the hall, Mark?"

"Of course," he says, and pushes the door open so we can walk through. He follows us in and closes the door. "Tell me what happened." Mark moves around behind his desk and sits down. Nancy sits down, too, but I don't. I just stand there.

Mark sits there without saying a word, looking straight at me, and I'm looking back at him and finally I say, "It was Jerry out there in the woods."

He gets up and comes back around the desk and wraps his arms around me, but I can't hug him back. He's still not talking, but eventually he lets go and turns to Nancy. "When did he find out?"

"We went out to get something to eat, and when we got back he said he felt like he needed to go back up and see if Tiny needed any more help. I guess he found out when he was up there."

"Mrs. Thompson," I say. They both turn and look at me and I say, "Mrs. Thompson told me. He had a wallet that didn't burn up. I guess when the docs were, you know, doing whatever, they found it and gave it to the police." I look at Mark and say, "Seems like they would have known that as soon as they found him."

"They might have known right away and hadn't told the next of kin yet, so they really couldn't tell anybody," Mark says and then stops. "Oh my God, Carrie. I need to tell Betty about this." He picks up the phone. When Mark says, "Oh my God," it sounds different than when anybody else says it. Like he's talking about a friend or something.

He hangs up and says, "Betty is on her way down here; she was in her office."

I look at Nancy and say, "I think I'm going back down to the house."

She nods and looks at Mark. "I'll stay with Boone for a while. You let us know when you talk to Carrie, okay?"

"I will. You take care of Boone."

I start to say that I don't need anybody to take care of me, but I just turn and start to open the door. It starts moving and I barely get my hand out of the way before Betty opens it and comes into the office.

She grabs me just like Mark did and I can tell she's been crying. "Oh, Boone, I just got off the phone with Carrie. That poor woman, she couldn't talk, she's just devastated. I wish she lived here in town, or in Knoxville. She's all by herself up there."

I'm betting that when she gets a chance to think about it she might be glad to be rid of him, but I don't say that.

"Listen, Betty, I was just going back down to the house. Nancy's going to stay with me."

She starts to say something and I catch her looking over at Mark. He's shaking his head, and she kind of shrugs and lets go of me. "You keep an eye on him, Nancy, okay?"

"I will, Betty."

"I know you didn't care for Jerry," she says to me, "but you and Carrie were always close. I don't want you to worry about her."

"I'm not worried about Carrie," I say. "Jerry was a real asshole. She's better off without him."

All three of them look at me without saying anything.

"What?" I say, getting a little mad at how they're staring at me. "He was. Ask anybody. Ask Nancy. Ask Carrie."

I look over at Nancy.

"I'm going to go check on Frankie."

I'm halfway out the door and stop. Pulling my sleeve up, I show them the scar and say, "This one came from Jerry trying to cut me one time. He was drunk on his ass and saying nasty stuff about Nancy, calling her a slut. He was doing that shit, so I had to fight him. He'd probably have killed me if Tiny hadn't showed up. I'm glad he's dead."

Nobody says anything for a second, and then Mark says, "You're a better man than this, Boone. I know you are. I'll be here when you're ready to talk about whatever's eating you up inside."

Right then I'm this close to telling him about Daddy, so I just about run out of the room and out the side door.

I hear them talking behind me but I can't tell what they're saying and I don't care. I'm halfway across the grass toward my place when Nancy catches up with me.

"Slow down, sweetie, I can't keep up."

I slow down a little and she comes up beside me.

"You going to start in on me too?" I say without looking over at her.

"No," she says, "I'm not. I was there, remember? I know you had to fight him. Don't mind Mark, he's a preacher, he has to say that stuff."

She's right, I know she is, and I slow down a little more. "I guess I didn't mean to talk that way about Carrie."

"I know that too."

Neither one of us says anything else until we get back to the house.

We sit down on the couch, Frankie right there with us, and after a minute Nancy says, "Well."

I don't say anything. She doesn't say it like it's a question, so I don't feel like I have to answer her back.

She takes a deep breath and says, "I don't know, Boone, I just don't know. . . .

"I've never felt this mixed up before. There's a part of me that's glad he's dead, I mean, there's a part that's hoping he suffered. I hate that, feeling like that. I've never felt this way about anybody before. I mean, you're not supposed to be glad somebody's dead, much less hope that they suffered. I want to feel bad that he died, and I just can't. The most I can do is feel bad for Carrie, and I do feel awful about her. Don't you feel bad for her, Boone?"

I shrug. "Yeah, I guess so. She was good to me, even tried to stand up to him a little. So yeah, I guess so."

"Do you think you ought to call her?"

I can't think of anything I want to say to her, and I think if I start talking about Jerry I'll say something that'll make her feel really bad. "I don't think I ought to do that."

Nancy is quiet for a minute and then says, "I bet you're right. Maybe in a day or two."

I don't think that's going to happen either, but I don't say so.

That thing Mark said the last time I saw Jerry alive, about him needing to talk to me, and say he was sorry or whatever, I keep thinking about that.

"Listen, can we talk about something else? I mean, anything else?"

"Sure, sweetie, what do you want to talk about?"

Now I'm stuck. I just sit there like I'm stupid and then I say, "So, what about you going off to school? When is that?"

I don't really want to talk about her going anywhere, but I keep thinking about Daddy, and Gamaliel, and now Jerry, and almost anything is better to think about than that. So I say, "Do you, like, move down there all in one day and then you're gone til next summer, or what?"

There is a long silence, and I look over at Nancy. She's staring at the wall across from us and not moving a muscle. Then she says, "It's funny, how Mom and Dad are so different about this. Dad, I can tell he's going to miss me, but he'd never say that, not in a million years. He's all, do this, don't do that, call if you need money, that kind of stuff.

"Mom is already packing even though it's seven or eight weeks until I can move. She's got all my cold weather stuff out and cleaned already and she got some boxes from the grocery store and has them full and taped up, ready to go. I was teasing her the other day, asking if she was trying to get rid of me, and she just started crying.

"She took me to the doctor two weeks ago and got me started on birth control pills. Dad would have a fit if he knew that, but she did it. I never thought she'd go behind his back like that, especially about, you know, sex." She's still not looking at me. "I'm not supposed to tell anybody about that, about the pills, I mean."

"How come she did that? The pills, I mean, not the packing."

I'm thinking about Nancy down there in Knoxville with all those college boys.

"Oh, she's just worried. I told her that she didn't need to, that I wasn't planning on getting all wild and stuff when I move out, but she just said, 'I know, honey, but just in case, you know.' I didn't tell her that the only boy I'm interested in is right here."

She's looking straight at me now and I think she might mean me but I don't know for sure, and I'm afraid to ask. And I can't keep looking at her, so I look over at Frankie.

Frankie is sitting right up next to Nancy and when I look at her she lays her head on Nancy's legs and looks up at me, waiting for me to give her a scratch or take her outside or anything that gets her some attention.

"When you were talking up there in Mark's office all I could think about is how you stood up for me," Nancy is talking real soft now, "even when he pulled that awful knife. I was so scared for you I didn't even care that he saw me with my shirt off, I didn't have anything else to give you to protect yourself."

I feel her hand on the back of my neck now, and it's so light and soft I can't hardly stand it.

"I mean, I'm glad Tiny showed up and all, but you were so brave, sweetie. You're the bravest man I know."

I can't think of the right thing to say or do here, so I just sit still and stare at Frankie.

She goes on, "I was telling Mom the truth, you know. I don't plan to go all crazy when I go to school, but when I am ready, I know exactly who I want to be with." She moves her hand up and down on my neck.

I think I'm supposed to be mad about her teasing me like this, but really I'm relieved, because I wouldn't know what to do if she was ready.

Then she gets up and goes over to the door and locks it.

Chapter Twenty-Six

I watch her walk back to the couch and when she sits down she says, "I don't want your housekeeper walking in on us."

"I don't have — " I start to say that she's not my housekeeper and I see Nancy grinning at me.

"Okay," I say. "I get it. It's kind of late in the afternoon anyway. She's usually here in the morning."

Nancy nods and leans back on the couch. She's right up next to me.

"I've thought a lot about that day up at Gamaliel's, when he pulled that knife on you," she says, and she reaches up and puts her hand on the side of my face. "About that, but more about what happened after Tiny was gone. I think about that part a lot."

She snuggles up against me and her hand drops from my face down to my chest. She whispers, "Do you ever think about that, Boone?"

I don't say anything out loud, but I think about that afternoon a lot too. I remember what Nancy looked like, what she felt like. It was the best few minutes I've ever had in my whole life. I squirm around and get my arm out from between us so I can put it around behind her.

"Yeah," I finally manage to say, but it comes out all scratchy, not smooth like on TV. "I think about it."

I pull her in closer and she raises her hand up to the back of my head, and when her arm moves up my hand is on her breast. I start to say sorry but she's not pushing me away. She's pulling my head down to hers and we're kissing and my hand stays right there.

Then she backs up a little and holds both her arms straight up. I remember from last time so I don't just sit there like an idiot. I grab her shirt at the bottom and pull it up over her head. As soon as I get it off she's grabbing hold of mine and I lean forward so she can get it over my head.

Then we're back together again and I'm trying to figure out the hooks. It's a different bra than the other time so it takes me a second, but I get it, and when I do she stops kissing me long enough to say, "Nice job, sweetie," and she takes hold of the front of it and then it's gone and we're kissing again. This time there's nothing between us.

A couple of times my hand brushes against the top of her jeans and both times she reaches down and moves it back up. I barely notice when it happens, everything else feels so good.

Then her whole body tenses up and she jerks straight, pushing away from me, and says, "What the hell?"

I don't know what's going on and start to say, "I'm not doing anything," but before I can, she starts laughing and says, "Frankie, you can't do that!"

She turns so she's back against the couch again and behind her, front paws up on the couch, is Frankie. She rubs her on the head and says, "You put that cold wet nose of yours right in the middle of my back, didn't you, girl?"

Frankie is real pleased with herself and Nancy is laughing and pretty soon so am I.

Even though it kind of ruins the mood, and I don't think we're getting back to where we were a minute ago. I'm feeling really good right now. Nancy stands up and gathers up her clothes and says, "I'm going to head on home if you're okay. You want me to stay a while longer, sweetie?"

I look at her standing there holding her clothes up to her chest and I think I've never seen a girl as beautiful as her, and I take a deep breath and say, "You're the most beautiful thing I've ever seen," and I can feel my face getting red.

She's getting red, too, and it's spreading down her neck and she doesn't say anything for a second. Then she drops her bra and shirt and grabs me so tight that I'm pressed up against her and I know she can feel me through our jeans and I'm holding her just as tight, and we stand there together and I wish it would last and last but I know it won't.

Sure enough, she eases up enough to lean back a little; she stares straight at me and I can see tears starting. Then she lets go and picks up her clothes again and runs out of the room. I hear the bedroom door close.

Then it opens again and she goes across the little hall into the bathroom. She doesn't close that door and I can see her looking at her face in the mirror. She wipes at it a few times and then comes back out.

"Do I look okay?" she asks.

"You look great," I say, and she laughs.

"I knew you'd say that, Boone, but I mean it. Do I need to fix my hair or anything?"

I step over to her and stand in front of her. I'm studying her face and she puts her hand on my chest and breathes real deep.

"Your cheeks are a little red," I tell her, "but your hair is fine."

"What's wrong with my cheeks?" she sounds worried.

"Nothing. I'm standing really close to you, is the only reason I can see it at all."

"Okay," she says. "You're sure?"

"Yeah," I say. "You were really a lot redder than this before, you know, I mean, just after we, we were . . . . Anyway, it'll probably go away in a few minutes." She's smiling now, and then gets serious.

"So, you never said. Do you need me to stay around for a while?"

"Nah, I'm okay. But you can stay here as long as you want to, you know?"

"I know that, sweetie. I told Mom just enough about what happened up at Tiny's to make her curious, so I'd better go tell her what I know. Well, some of what I know anyway."

As long as she doesn't tell anybody about how that still got up there.

Chapter Twenty-Seven

It's a couple of days before I have to think about Jerry again, and it's because of Carrie. I look out the window up the hill toward the main building and Mark and Carrie are walking down toward me.

As soon as I see her I think about seeing Jerry. First in the woods all burned up, and then those other times, at Gamaliel's funeral, at his old house with that knife in his hand, standing in our old house with that tire iron, but mostly him dead in the woods and that makes me think of Daddy and I'm mad before they even get to the door. I don't want to talk to anybody and I sure don't want to have to deal with whatever it is Mark's bringing down here.

I try to remember the last time I was face to face with Carrie and I think it must have been the funeral, when Mark got me up there to talk about Gamaliel. Anyway, it's been a while and the last I remember about her was her throwing me out of Gamaliel's house even though he said I could stay there. Betty and I were standing right about where I am now and she told me that Carrie was getting ready to sell the place or something and I was going to have to leave and did I need a place to stay for a while. I try to remember it wasn't Carrie's doing, it was Jerry being an asshole like usual, and that doesn't really help much at all.

One of them knocks on the door and Frankie is up and staring at it, but she doesn't growl or bark or anything. I think about not answering, but I know Mark and I know he'd just keep on pounding until I let them in. He's got some mule in him, and I figure I might as well get this over with, whatever it is.

I open up the door and Mark is standing there. Carrie's a little behind him and she's looking at the window and the trees and everywhere but at me.

"Hi, Boone, can we come in?"

He waits for a second and finally I swing the door open and say, "Okay, come on."

I don't like how this feels. Carrie won't look at me and I remember enough about her to know something is bad wrong. If Mark is bringing her here it must have something to do with me, but I don't know what it might be. We haven't had anything to do with each other since she used Betty to tell me to get out of Gamaliel's house.

When I think about that, about how she had Betty do her dirty work for her and about all the stuff I did for her, helping her with Gamaliel, dealing with Jerry when he was such an asshole, when I think about all that, I start getting mad and so when Mark starts talking I'm already not wanting to hear anything he has to say about Carrie.

He makes it a lot worse when he says, "Carrie has something she feels like she needs to say, and I thought I ought to be here when she says it." He turns his head a little and nods at Carrie. "Go ahead, Carrie."

I look over at her and her fists are real tight and her face is red, and for a long time she doesn't say anything and when she does it's like a shout. "It's your fault, Boone Hammond, it's your fault!"

I start to open my mouth and she cuts me off before I can say anything.

"He came down here twice to try to make amends to you! He'd stopped drinking, he was trying to make things right with everybody, and you, you treated him just like dirt, worse than that, he got into that damn meth because he couldn't stand you treating him like that and now he's dead and it's all your fault!" and she's almost screaming at me now.

By now I'm real mad and Mark can tell, and he sees it's not going to end up like he wanted it to, so he jumps in before I can say anything. "Now, Carrie, we talked about this, you and me. Remember? Maybe we ought to talk a little more before you try to talk to

Boone here. Why don't we go on back up to my office?"

"I was trying so hard, and he was trying, too, and he was doing so well, and then he came down here and it all went to hell, every bit of it!" She's crying now and I'm so mad I could punch her right in the face. She's got no right coming in here talking to me like that.

Frankie knows something is going on but she can't figure it out. She knows I'm mad at Carrie, but she's always liked Carrie and she doesn't know what to do. She ends up standing right next to me and I can feel how tense she is. She'd jump if I told her to, and I've got half a mind to tell her to.

Mark's talking fast, working as hard as he can to get her out of the house but she's damn near out of control now, and he finally has to almost pick her up and carry her out the door. As soon as they're out I slam the door and go over to the window. He's got her walking now and they're on their way back up to the main building.

"Can you believe that shit?" I ask Frankie. She's calming back down now that Carrie's out of the house and looks up at me and tries a wag or two. I give her a scratch on top of her head and she's fine.

I'm not fine at all. I'm still pissed.

Funny how the first thing I think of is that I ought to call Nancy. I decide to wait on that and head

225

to the kitchen to make an S&S, a real strong one. I think if Mark hadn't been here I'd have probably thrown her out on her ass, talking to me that way. She's better off without that piece of shit.

I'm about done with the S&S and mostly calmed down, thinking about making another one or giving Nancy a call, when there's another knock on the door. I really don't want to have anything to do with anybody right now, so I just sit there. Whoever it is knocks again.

"Boone? It's me, Mark. Just me. I know you're still in there, Boone. Open up."

I'm not surprised that he came back. The only question was when, and I figured that would depend on how quick he could get rid of Carrie. It was middle of the morning when they came busting in on me and it's not quite lunch time yet, so he must have been quick.

"Come on, Boone, I need to make sure you're okay. Let me in."

"I'll be there in a minute," I say, and go into the kitchen. I pour a little shine into the glass and drink it straight. It almost chokes me, but I shake my head a few times and get out the Thunderstorm from the fridge. I fill up the glass and carry it to the door with me and open it.

Mark is standing out in the yard looking up at the sky. He turns around when he hears the door and says, "I'm sorry, Boone, I didn't know she was going to unload on you like that."

I wave the glass at him and say, "I figured that out already. You want to come in and have a Thunderstorm?"

He looks at me kind of funny for a second and then says, "Sure, Boone, if you don't mind."

I don't mind at all, but when he says that it makes me think about Daddy, about how he'd never invite a black man into his house, or a Mexican either. Not that anybody ever came to our house, everybody knew Daddy had a temper and I don't guess Momma had any friends. But the way Mark said that, it reminded me of him.

Of course right now pretty much everything reminds me of Daddy.

Mark comes in and sits down. I keep going, into the kitchen, and say, "You want a big glass or a little one?"

"Just a little, Boone, I've got something I've got to do in a few minutes. Like I said, I wanted to see if you were okay. Carrie really went after you."

He stops then like I'm supposed to say something, but I don't. I hand him his glass and sit down. He's where Nancy was before and I'm in my place. Frankie's over on her bed watching us.

"You know what happened to Jerry wasn't your fault," Mark starts out, and I cut him off, because I don't want to talk about Jerry right now. Or ever.

"Hell, I know that, Mark, I don't know what she was talking about. I didn't make him a drunk, didn't make him stop drinking, didn't show him where to get meth, didn't set him on fire." It's like I can't stop talking now that I'm started. I take a deep breath and a sip of Thunderstorm. "What the hell was wrong with her anyway? She knows better than me or you or anybody what an asshole Jerry was. I mean, he — " I have to stop myself from talking before I say something stupid, so I lean back against the cushion and take another sip.

"I just wanted to tell you it's not your — "

"I know that, I told you that!" I don't mean to shout at Mark but I can tell by the look on his face that that's what I'm doing. I start over.

"I'm fine, Mark, fine, I just didn't appreciate her yelling at me like that."

"Pretty sure you're not fine, Boone, but I know better than to push you on this. You let me know when you're ready to tell me what's really going on," Mark says, real soft.

He gets up. "Thanks for the Thunderstorm, Boone. I have to leave, but you know where I am. I can promise you it'll do you good to tell somebody what's eating at you. Doesn't have to be me, but it can be if you want." He starts into the kitchen and I stand up real quick.

"I'll take care of the glass, Mark, you go do whatever you got to do."

He just stands there for a minute and then nods, hands me the glass, and heads to the door. "I'll see you around, Boone. Let me know when you've got more stuff from the residents here."

I don't answer him and he says, "Goodbye, Frankie, keep an eye on him, okay?" and he's gone.

In the kitchen I set his glass in the sink and mine on the counter, mix another S&S and drink it standing there. I don't even care that I'm going to run low pretty quick like this.

He kept saying it wasn't my fault. Why did he do that, over and over? It wasn't my fault, Jerry wasn't, Trevor's mom wasn't, Daddy wasn't, Gamaliel wasn't. Hell, I'd even saved Gamaliel once, when I found him in his back yard. So I know he wasn't my fault.

He was just old.

I go sit down on the couch and I'm asleep in about five seconds, even though it's the middle of the day.

When I wake up it's getting dark outside and I'm hungry as hell. There's nothing in the fridge, I know, but I go check it anyway. The clock on the stove says it's after eight, so the cafeteria is out except for fruit and crackers and shit like that.

229

"Frankie, I'm going to go get a hamburger or something. You stay here, I'll bring you one, okay?"

There's a drive-through not too far up the highway; I head over there and they've got one of those specials, two hamburgers for $6.00, so I get that and take them home, give one to Frankie, and eat the other one sitting on the couch with the TV on. Another show about rich people sitting around all day not doing a damn thing except talking to each other.

I wish Nancy was here.

Chapter Twenty-Eight

The next day I take Frankie up to the benches outside the main building and let everybody see her. It hasn't been that long, but they haven't seen her since she got back from the vet, so I tell the story of how she got shot a bunch of times. Every time I tell it shorter and shorter because I'm already tired of talking about it.

Melvin is there with a bunch of books beside him like usual, and I stop at his bench last. I start to tell him the short version of what happened to Frankie and he holds up one hand.

"You don't need to tell me that, Boone, you already did, right after it happened. I've been watching you going around and I would estimate you've told this story a dozen times already. Why don't we talk about something else?"

He puts his hand down at his side and snaps his fingers. "Come over here and say hi, Frankie. Are you feeling better?"

As soon as Frankie hears her name she's all excited and comes wiggling over to Melvin. He laughs and pats his thigh and she puts her head right there and looks up at him like he's the greatest guy ever lived. I don't mind too much, though; she's that way around most everybody, unless they're bad people. She can tell, usually before anybody else, about that kind of thing.

"Your dog has excellent taste, young man," Melvin says.

I have to laugh at that. "Yeah, I guess you're right, Melvin."

He looks away from her and up at me. "How are you, Boone? Last time I saw you was just after you took Frankie to the vet, and you were worried sick."

I nod. "I'm good now, thanks for asking. Once I got Frankie back, you know ...."

"I do indeed. Did I ever tell you about my dog Eleanor?"

The first thing I think is that's a weird name for a dog, but I just say, "I don't think you did."

He leans back on the bench. "It was a long time ago. I wasn't much older than you are now.

"That would have been in the mid-60's," he says after looking out across to the woods for a long time. "I was living in Charleston then, actually on Folly Beach, right on the Atlantic. I was working in restaurants then, waiting tables, spending my money as fast as I got it, smoking and drinking and lying on the beach looking at the sea and the sky. Not a care in the world.

"One of the restaurant managers had a dog, a Labrador, black as midnight, that got loose once when she was in heat and came back pregnant. He had no idea what breed the father was, so he was giving away the puppies. Up until then I hadn't even thought about getting a dog."

I'm looking at Frankie while he's talking, so I don't notice right away why he stops talking. When I look up at him he has tears in his eyes.

"I named her after the Beatles song "Eleanor Rigby," for no good reason except that I liked it. She was the one constant in my life for, I don't know, six or seven years."

I don't want to ask, but it seems like I ought to. "What happened to her, Melvin?"

"Car hit her," he says, and his voice is different than I've ever heard it before. It's so sad it almost makes me cry, especially when I think about losing Frankie.

He starts coughing then and I'm about to call somebody when he stops and shakes his head. "Let's change the subject, shall we?"

I nod.

"Tell me what you've been up to, Boone. I mean besides Frankie and the vet."

So I tell him about the fire and that gets him started on a story about when he was working for the National Park Service and had to help the firefighters during the season, mostly just making sure they had food and water for whenever they could take a quick break.

He talks enough for me to get a good story for Mark and besides, it sounds like something I might like to do. The Park Service, I mean, not the fire fighting. I had enough of that up at Tiny's to do me. I decide to ask Mark if he knows about how that kind of thing works. The Smokies are right here, and I know how to be in the woods. I'll ask him.

Then I think, how stupid is that, Boone? You're standing right in front of somebody that used to do it for real, and you're thinking about asking a preacher that probably doesn't know anything about it. Not that I know anything about Mark's story. For all I know, he might have been one of those Navy SEALs that Tiny was talking about.

I open my mouth to ask Melvin about how you get to work for the Park Service and about that time one of the staff comes up and says it's time for him to go in. Some kind of doctor's appointment.

Mark is out under the tree next to the chapel a couple of days later and I go up to him and say, "I've got another story from Melvin. Two, I guess, I've got two stories, but one of them's pretty short."

He tells me to sit down and I do, and Frankie sits down between us so she can get a scratch from either one of us. I tell him about Melvin's dog, which doesn't take long at all, and then about him working for the Park Service, and when I say that it sounds like something I might want to look at he gets all excited and promises he'll check on it. Then he looks at me and grins.

"You know that would be the end of you sleeping until the day's half gone, right?"

"To tell you the truth, I'm getting kind of tired of that, Mark. I mean, there's nothing on TV worth a damn, and all I do when I stay up late is go round and round the channels."

Chapter Twenty-Nine

Melvin has the best stories, but I spend the next couple of days talking to some of the other old folks, since that's what I'm supposed to be doing to get to stay here. Mrs. Reston is still waiting for the visit from her grandchild that hasn't happened yet and I'm pretty sure it never will. Mr. Vandergriff is a little friendlier than before, but it's only if I'm out by myself. If I've got Frankie with me, which is most of the time, he won't even wave at me.

So I end up at Melvin's bench pretty much every day. I plan it out so he's the last stop, so if he really gets going I can get one good long story or a few short ones. Today he's back on the beach at Charleston.

"You need to add that to your list of places to go, Boone," he says, looking from me to Frankie and back. "It's a great town, at least it was then, full of history if you like that kind of thing and the food there is fantastic. Seafood right out of the ocean."

I don't care much about history or seafood, but if I was to be fair about it, the only fish I've ever had besides trout or catfish is fish sandwiches with those square things that don't have any taste at all. I'd take fried catfish over that any day, but I don't say that to Melvin. He's still talking.

"There's a part of town that's right on the ocean, they call it the Battery, and some of the gardens behind the houses are a couple of hundred years old. Absolutely gorgeous."

We had a garden, but I don't get the hundred year old part at all. You pick through it every year and then plow it under for next spring. I start to ask Melvin about that when he changes the subject.

"So when are you going to Memphis? That really should be your first trip, you know."

I don't hear him at first because now I'm thinking about a little patch right out next to the kitchen door that Momma had, there was a scrawny rosebush that looked like it was about to die but it never did and a bunch of, what was it she called them, Black-Eyed Susans, that would almost strangle that rosebush every year and spread out into the yard, too. She couldn't keep them beat back. I'm thinking about those Black-Eyed Susans and Melvin asks again.

"When are you going to Memphis, Boone?"

"What?"

"You know, Memphis. Birthplace of the blues. Elvis. Beale Street. Ribs and pulled pork. When are you going?"

I say the first thing that comes into my head. "If I can't take Frankie with me I'm not going anywhere."

Melvin looks at me, and then at Frankie and back to me. "Well, now, that's an issue. I can see where that might be a problem. Lots of places won't allow pets, you know, in motel rooms and such."

He doesn't say anything else for a few minutes, and I'm thinking about Momma and Hannah and Aunt Claire and how she wanted me to take the damn bus to Memphis and I know they wouldn't let Frankie on the bus, and then Melvin says, "Of course you could camp out along the way, if you went the right time of year. Get a camper top for that truck of yours and you could go anywhere you wanted to go. And Frankie could go right along with you."

That piece of shit truck wouldn't make it to the next county, much less Memphis, however far that is, and I tell Melvin so.

"You sure about that?"

"I'm pretty sure, yeah," I say, and I'm wondering why everybody is pushing me to go to Memphis.

Melvin is getting all excited now, and he ignores what I'm trying to tell him about the truck, and he says, "I've got a road map of the country in my room. I'll mark a half a dozen places you really ought to see and bring it out here in a day or so. You'll love it, I promise."

He starts listing places and getting more and more worked up, and finally I tell him I need to go, and stand up. Frankie is ready to move; she's been sitting for a while now.

He grabs my hand. "I'm going to take care of this right away, Boone. Oh, how I envy you! You've got all these places that will be brand new to you, and some of them are nothing like around here."

I'm thinking around here is okay with me, but I know Melvin well enough to know there's no stopping him. He's going to do this no matter what I say.

The next day I tell Mark about what Melvin's working on and he thinks it's a great idea. Then he stops and says, "I thought you wanted to go to work for the Park Service."

"Mark, I'm just telling you what Melvin said. I'm not going to do it. That truck would never make a trip like he's talking about."

"Why don't you get your friend Tiny to take a look at it? He can tell you what kind of shape it's in, I'll bet, and what you'd have to do to make it reliable."

I would like to take a drive down to Knoxville every now and then. I don't think that would be too much for the truck, but I know Daddy never took care of it, and I almost never drive it anywhere, except to the store and back. If I went to work anywhere but here, and here's not really work, it's more charity, and that's starting to bother me a lot, if I worked anywhere else, I'd need some kind of truck to drive back and forth and around if I had to do that for the job.

"I might do that, Mark. Talk to Tiny, I mean."

"Good. I think that's a really good idea. I've been thinking about your interest in the Park Service, and if you're still interested, I can ask around."

It's a couple of days before I get around to calling Tiny, and Mrs. Thompson is the one who picks up the phone.

"Hello, Mrs. Thompson, is Tiny around anywhere?"

"Is this Boone?"

"Yes, ma'am, it is."

"Well, it's good to hear from you, Boone. We sure did appreciate your help during the fire. Wasn't that awful about that man Jerry? Tiny said you knew him a little."

Every time I tell people how much better off Carrie is without that guy they give me a hard time, so I just say, "Yeah, I knew him some. Y'all didn't have any damage from that fire, did you?"

"It never even got on our land, but it was a close thing. We sure do — oh, wait a minute, here's Phillip coming in. Phillip, it's Boone on the phone for you!"

She's shouting this last part, but not into the phone, and in a minute Tiny says, "Hey, Boone."

"Hey. listen, Tiny, I was wondering if you could take a look at my piece of shit truck. It's running okay right now, but if I decide I want to go more than to the store and back I don't want to end up on the side of the road somewhere."

"Can't do it today, but I got nothing going on tomorrow. Why don't you bring it on up here and we'll take a look?"

"I'll do that. See you then. You thinking morning or afternoon?"

"I'd rather it be after lunch if that works for you."

"Sounds good."

The next day I take Frankie and head up to Tiny's place. He's out next to the building we cleared out and when I get there I see some shelves that weren't there before.

"Like my new shop?" he says.

I step inside and look around. It's pretty small, but he's got a lot of tools in here.

"Long as you're in there, bring out that worklight and plug it in next to the door there."

The only thing that looks like a light is a bulb inside a metal cage, and it has a long cord, so I grab that and take it to him. He's already got the hood up and hangs the light from a brace so he can see whatever it is he's going to work on. Frankie is out in the yard with Eunuch and they're wearing each other out, round and round.

"So what brought this on?" Tiny says, pulling out the dipstick and holding it under the light.

"Nothing really, I just thought if I wanted to go to Knoxville, or, you know, Memphis, I'd want to be able to make it there and back."

He slides the dipstick back into the engine. "Memphis? Why do you want to go there? There's an awful lot of those, you know, African-Americans in Memphis. Whole city's full of them. Might be kind of dangerous for a skinny white boy from out in the sticks."

It's hard for me to get mad at Tiny, even when he does this kind of shit, so I hold my arm in a kind of a V shape across my chest, making a fist, and tense up my muscles and say, "You see that? Tell me that doesn't scare you right out of your skin."

He laughs out loud and pokes at my arm with his finger. "I got to admit I'm pretty terrified, Boone."

I nod and say, "That's right. Plus I'll have Frankie. If we have to kick any ass we'll do it."

Tiny's shaking his head and grinning, and I say, "Actually, I don't see me going anywhere near that far, but this guy Melvin at the home, he's lived all over the place, he tells me I need to get out and see someplace besides here."

Tiny doesn't say anything to that and I say, "I'm a lot more likely to go down to Knoxville after Nancy moves down there for school."

"You talk to her lately?"

"No, not in a day or two."

"Maybe you ought to give her a call," Tiny says.

He keeps working, but I'm just standing there staring at him. Finally I say, "Now why would you say that?"

He shrugs. "I heard that her plans were changing, is all. Her mom and my mom are, well, they're not good friends, but they talk every now and then. Mom ran into her at the store yesterday, and when she got back she didn't tell me everything, but I got the idea that things were pretty tense over at Nancy's house."

"Tense like how?"

"I don't know," he says, pulling off a wire. "Go get me a spark plug wrench, will you?"

I go into the shop and look around for a while until Tiny sticks his head in the door and points. "Right there."

He goes through the spark plugs and looks at all the hoses and belts and stuff and checks the mileage, and then he says, "I think this truck's good for somebody with a farm that wants something to haul wood and hay and pull a trailer down to the lumber store and stuff like that. I don't know that I'd take it on a trip."

"That's what I thought."

"Want me to keep an eye out for somebody that wants one?"

I look at him. "You serious? Somebody might want this thing? For how much?"

"Well," he says, "the tires are about half gone, and it's going to need brakes before too long, and it's got a bunch of miles on it, but right now it runs okay. I'd say now's the time to sell it, before something big happens and it's no good for anything but parts."

"But how much?"

"I don't know, Boone, you might get a couple of thousand for it, but probably not. It's more like a fifteen hundred dollar truck, is what I think,"

"Okay, so how much would a decent truck cost?"

"You mean one like Mom's?"

I look at him like he's a damn fool and then realize he's kidding. I'm getting better at that, figuring that out.

"Yeah, Tiny, just like hers."

"I'd say no more than $45,000, unless you wanted those heated seats. Mom's always complaining about cold seats in the winter."

"Well, okay then. I better start saving up."

"Now," he says, "if I was interested in selling that one," and he points to a truck I've seen him in off and on, "which I'm not, I'd probably want $8,000. It's ten, no, I guess it's eleven years old now, and it's pretty clean. If it was beat up I'd not get more than six for it."

"So this piece of shit and $4,000 would get me a pretty good truck."

"It would if you were a good trader. It would definitely get me a good one, because I'm an excellent trader."

Chapter Thirty

On the way home I'm thinking about all kinds of stuff.

I never thought about selling this truck, guess I didn't think anybody would give money for it. What Tiny said makes sense, though, and I'm thinking about that money in the bank. I could get a real truck.

If I had a truck I could go to Memphis, or Charleston, or any of those places Melvin was talking about. That whole idea is kind of scary. It'd mean leaving here, and here's the only place I've ever been. I don't know anything about being anywhere else.

When I think about it, though, there's not much here I care about. Gamaliel's gone, Momma's gone, Nancy's moving away real soon, and that just leaves Mark and Tiny. Mark cares about me because he's a preacher and that's his job, and Tiny, well, I'd hate to lose him, but who knows what he's going to do? Hannah doesn't even live here, and I don't see

Momma coming back here even if she could. She might go stay with Aunt Claire and Hannah, but she's not coming back here for me. I mean, where would she come back to? That old house she and Daddy and all of us lived in is probably half on the ground by now, and I don't really have anyplace to live. Betty is letting me live in that little house, but she's just being nice because Jerry had screwed me over so bad. The still's a pile of ashes, except for what the law took with them, so that's not really keeping me here, plus I don't know how I feel about starting that up again without the old man. No, there is not much here.

I think mainly it's me and Frankie, and we might as well be anywhere. There is one other thing, though.

The thing about Nancy, what Tiny said, is bothering me a lot. I try to call as soon as I get home and the phone rings for a long time and then somebody says, "Hi."

"Can I talk to Nancy?"

"Is this Boone?"

"Yeah. Who is this?"

"This is Cyrus. Nancy can't talk right now."

He sounds like he can't wait to get off the phone.

"Listen, Cyrus, is everything okay up there?"

There's a long silence and then he says, "Why would you ask me that? Somebody say something?"

247

I don't answer right away and he hangs up on me.

What the hell is going on here? I wonder if Stan is mad about something and he's got everybody tiptoeing around like we all used to do with Daddy. Stan's a lot richer than Daddy ever was, and smarter, and has lots better, well, everything, but some of the stuff he's done and some of the stuff I've seen at their house sure reminds me of Daddy.

Then I think, oh shit, what if he found out about the birth control pills? That would do it. He'd go right through the roof. He'd be pretty mad at Nancy and really mad at her mom. I decide to try Nancy's cell phone.

Somebody answers but doesn't say anything, so I say, "Nancy?"

There's a real short pause and then Stan says, "Who the hell is this? Whoever you are, don't call this number again! You understand?" and he hangs up.

Oh, man. He sounds like he's just looking for somebody to beat up. It's got to be the pills. He's not even letting her answer her own phone. There is no way he's going to let her even go off to the store now, much less college. I wonder if he's tearing the place up. I know Daddy would. He'd be throwing stuff and breaking stuff, whatever glass he was drinking out of, everything.

I spend the rest of the day at the house, hoping Nancy will call or come by, even though I know that if I'm right there is no chance in hell I'm going to see her for a while.

If Stan is like Daddy, he'll find something else to be mad about sooner or later, but Hannah wasn't ever old enough for Daddy to be mad about this kind of thing. So I don't know. I know one thing; if I went up there right now, he'd shoot me if he had a gun. He might not even let me get out of the truck.

Then I think, what if it was a different truck?

If it was a different truck, he wouldn't do anything until I got out and he saw who it was. So that's no good.

Dammit, I need to talk to Nancy about all this stuff, about getting a truck, working for the park, going on this trip Melvin wants me to go on, and her going off to college, and about Momma and Hannah and all that.

So when I wake up the next morning I end up going to see Mark. I got to talk to somebody about this, and I don't know when I'll see Nancy again. I don't even know what's going on up at her house, I might be making all this up, but I don't think I am.

Mark looks real busy when I stick my head in his door. "Hi, Boone, how's it going?"

Then he puts down the papers he's looking at and says, "What's wrong?"

"Listen, you got a minute?"

He looks at his desk and then at his watch. "If this is important, it would be better if I could finish up some stuff. You want to go out and get some lunch somewhere? I'll let you drive the Mini."

I shrug and say, "Yeah, lunch is good. See you in about an hour and a half."

"Okay," he says, looking right at me. "You sure you can wait that long?"

"Yeah, I can wait. No big deal."

I turn to leave and almost knock Mrs. Reston down.

"Young man, why are you not in school?"

It's the same question she always asks me.

"I'm done with school, Mrs. Reston, remember?"

She nods. "Of course. Would you excuse me? I have an appointment and you're standing in the doorway."

I turn around and look at Mark. He gives me a little smile and says, "Boone was just coming by to make an appointment himself, Mrs. Reston. Why don't you come on in?"

When it's about time to go, I check Frankie's food and water and say, "I'm going to meet with Mark for a while, girl. I'll be back real soon."

She's awful good about me leaving her alone, as long as I don't do it too often or for too long a time. She watches me head toward the door and when I turn back to look at her one more time she's circling

250

around on her blanket. She lies down with her nose pointed toward the door. I close it and head on up to Mark's office.

"Thanks for waiting, Boone," he says when I get to his door. "Mrs. Reston almost never asks to see me, so I thought it might be important."

"So what's going on with her?"

He gives me a look. "You know I can't talk about that, Boone, it's private, and part of my job here is to be somebody these people can come to and not worry about what they say getting spread all over the place."

"Does that include me?"

"Of course it does," he says, very seriously. "You can talk to me about anything. There are, however, some things I can't keep private, you know."

I don't know and I tell him that.

"Oh," he says, "it's like most professions. If somebody reports abuse, something that puts people in danger, I can't keep that secret. Most things people tell me are things I can keep between them and me, and that's what I do. But there are limits."

That's good to know, I think to myself. Wonder if I told him about the moonshine if he'd have to tell. Daddy and what happened to him, I'm pretty sure about that one. He'd have to tell that. Nancy and the pills, he could probably keep that secret. I got to figure out how to ask him about all this stuff before I tell him anything.

What I can talk about is the truck and the trips Melvin wants me to take and how there's nothing here that's holding on to me except that this is where I've always been. So that's what I start with, after he pulls out of the parking lot and onto the road.

"So Melvin has this idea about me taking some kind of trip and taking Frankie along with me, and he's all excited about it and has a map he's going to give me with a lot of places marked on it. He keeps saying that I need to go see all these places while I'm young and how he wishes he could go with me and I don't know, Mark, to tell you the truth it kind of scares me a little."

I would never have told Daddy that I was scared of anything. He would have called me a pussy and a baby and it would have been a month before he stopped making fun of me, if he ever did stop. Telling Mark was not something I meant to do, it just slipped out. But now it's out there and I'm waiting for him to say something.

He's right in the middle of a long curve and waits until he straightens the car out before he says anything. "It's been a while since I was your age, Boone, but I can still remember the first time I went out on my own, I mean really went out. Left town, didn't plan to come back to my parent's house, I was stepping out into the world and I tell you I was scared to death. At least part of me was, and the other part couldn't wait to get going. Do you have that part in you somewhere?"

"I don't know. I guess so." As soon as he says that about being excited, I realize that I do feel a little bit of that. "Hadn't really thought about that part of it."

"Well, I think having those conflicting feelings is pretty normal, so it sounds like you're right where you ought to be. Have you thought about all the details? What are you going to do for money, do you trust that truck to get you where you want to go, where are you going to stay, stuff like that?"

I tell him that Tiny might be helping me find a better truck and he looks at me kind of strange and finally says, "You have money to buy a truck, Boone? I have to say I'm kind of surprised at that."

"It won't be a new truck or anything like that, but Tiny says I might get one or two thousand for my old truck and I've got a little money put back. Momma sent me some there at first before Jake made her stop, and I don't spend anything, really, so what Betty gives me I've still got most of that."

Mark doesn't say anything and I keep going.

"He says that my truck is good for a farm truck, and I need something that I can count on. We haven't looked or anything, but if I could find something, me and Frankie could sleep in the back. Maybe I could make some money along the way, you know, doing some kind of jobs."

We get to a place Mark's been telling me about, where they have hot sandwiches and pizzas and hamburgers. He pulls into the lot and we go inside.

"I think you and I should sit down and talk seriously about money if you're planning to make this trip," Mark says, looking at the menu. The waiter comes over and he gets something called a Philly cheese steak and I say, "Are those any good?"

The waiter answers before Mark has a chance to say anything. "It's our best seller, sir. Delicious."

"Okay," I say, "I'll have one too then."

When he's gone Mark says, "I just think you ought to take your time on this, Boone. It might be the best thing in the world for you, getting away from here, but you don't need to do it tomorrow."

He's right, I know he is, so I say, "There's some other stuff I wanted to talk to you about."

Chapter Thirty-One

"Okay," he says. "Like what?"

"If I don't do this trip, and I might not, you know, at least not right now, I thought I might try to get some work up in the park. You know anything about that?"

"I know that even if you didn't get a job in the park, if you go up into Sevier County there's all kinds of jobs. They're always needing people, especially during the tourist season."

"So how does that work?"

About that time the waiter comes up with two huge sandwiches and puts them in front of us. "Enjoy!" he says, and heads off toward another table.

"You go get an application, fill it out, and wait for them to call you. Some jobs require more than others. If you're wanting to get started with the Park Service, for instance, you'll need to have at least a high school diploma . . . ." He stops talking and looks at me.

"You never graduated, did you, Boone?"

I shake my head. My mouth is full of food. This is a really good sandwich.

"That's going to make it a lot harder for you as far as jobs go," he says, "I'll have to give that some thought."

I don't want to talk about this any more. This is turning into more of a hassle than it's worth. Maybe I ought to just forget about the whole job thing.

Seems like Mark has figured that out, because he says, "Let's talk about something else, Boone. How are you feeling? Carrie really laid into you the other day."

I don't really want to talk about Carrie either. I want to talk about Nancy.

"I'm fine. Listen, I'm kind of worried about Nancy."

He sits up a little. "Why is that? Has something happened?"

So I tell him about not being able to get hold of Nancy and how Stan yelled into the phone when I tried her cell and I say, "There's one more thing that I know but it's a secret and I don't know whether or not I can tell you."

"Oh," he says, "so that's what that whole thing with Mrs. Reston was about. Let me ask you this. Is it about somebody being hurt or hurting somebody else?"

I shake my head.

"Does it involve children?"

I shake my head again.

He sits back in his chair. "Then I think I can keep your secret, Boone. We do have some choice about this kind of thing, but what I just asked you about, that stuff we don't have any choice at all. You understand?"

"Yeah, I get that."

"So, what's this about?"

I tell him that he can't tell anybody, but that Nancy just got a prescription for birth control pills and I think her dad found out about it.

"How did she get it?"

"Her mom helped her get it, is what she told me."

"Well, I think if I was her dad and found out about this right before she went off to college, I'd be mad too."

We sit and eat for a minute and then I say, "She's not, you know, doing it. She told me she wasn't ready."

Mark grins. "She told you that, did she?"

"Yeah."

"Sounds like she cares a lot about what you think, Boone. What did you say to her when she said that?"

"I don't remember saying anything. She, she stayed for a little while and then went on home."

Mark laughs out loud and I look at him like, what the hell are you laughing at? This isn't funny. He sees my expression and waves his hand at me.

"I'm not laughing at you, Boone, I'm laughing at what a good thing this is. Your Nancy is a fine young woman, I hope you know that. You're lucky to have her in your life."

"I know that, Mark."

"So," he says, "what do you think of the Philly cheese steak?"

I wave my hand over my empty plate.

"That's what I think, too. You know, if you take this trip Melvin is trying to talk you into, you could go to Philadelphia and get a real Philly cheese steak."

I don't have any idea where Philadelphia is.

This whole conversation with Mark, I don't know about it. It's gone all over the place and I'm not sure I feel any better than when we got in his car. I got a good meal out of it and he let me drive when we headed back, but sometimes when I talk to him I feel better. This time it doesn't help as much.

I don't try Nancy for a couple of days, but I do talk to Tiny about the whole truck thing.

"My family," he says, "is a Chevy family all the way." We're sitting on the tailgate of my piece of shit truck and he waves his hand at the side of the house where everybody parks. It's all Chevy. There's his mom's truck, a Suburban, and Tiny's truck.

"Those folks that live kind of across from where you used to live, they're Ford people. They wouldn't ever even think about buying a Chevrolet, and if you married into that family you'd sure have to sell your Honda or your Dodge or whatever if you didn't already have a Ford.

"My family is not that bad, but they're close. I've been thinking about your truck and what you might be able to get for five thousand or so, and I've got a couple of ideas. Nothing I'd buy for myself, you know, because I'm still living here and that limits my choices, but if you were to find a Toyota, about 1995 or 1996, they say the only thing that ever wears out on those trucks is the seat cushions. They run forever. I wouldn't walk away from a Chevy either, but that's because I know that brand real well."

"So are you gonna help me do this?"

"What, you mean buy a truck?"

"Yeah, man, I don't know shit about that kind of thing. I'd get screwed sure as the sun comes up in the morning. You've done this before, plus anybody'd be scared to cheat you."

He laughs. "If you'd grow about four inches and put on a few pounds, maybe they'd be scared of you too."

Chapter Thirty-Two

The next time I see Melvin he waves me over. He looks real excited.

"I've been working on this ever since we talked last," he says, and holds a folded map out to me. "Come on over to this table and spread it out. I'll talk you through what I have so far."

He gets up and walks across the sidewalk to one of those round concrete tables and sits on a bench. I follow him over and unfold the map. It's a map of the whole country, but the only part marked up is the lower right.

"I think you should start in the South," he says, and I haven't heard him sound like this before. His voice is louder and he's talking kind of fast. "There's so much to see without even leaving this country, but in the South you'd be on more or less familiar ground. Now, if you start by heading west you ought to make a stop in Nashville, but Memphis is the real thing. You have to go there.

"I would recommend that you go south from Memphis to New Orleans. It's like no other city around, unless you go to Europe. The French Quarter has food and drink and music, jazz and blues and it goes on all night long. From there you ought to go east, maybe stop in Biloxi before you hit Florida and head for the Keys.

"You have never seen anything like the Everglades, Boone. The road through it is straight, only has one curve, and the land is flat as a pool table. The Keys are great too, and if you make it all the way to Key West, you've got nothing in front of you but ocean until you get to Cuba or South America.

"If you don't want to go that far the first time out you can go straight east from New Orleans to St. Augustine, Florida and then turn north. You come to Savannah first and then Charleston, and you can keep going right up the coast or head back inland, angle up through the Smokies, and you're back here."

He's pointing to all this stuff on the map and I can tell he's real excited about it all, but I don't understand a bunch of what he's talking about. He's about to talk me out of it by dumping all this on me at once, and it's like he figures that out while he's talking because he stops for a minute and then leans back away from the map.

"Sorry, Boone, I got kind of carried away there, didn't I?" He looks at me and I don't say anything, but he sort of half smiles and says, "I thought so."

When I tell him that unless I get another truck I won't be going anywhere but maybe Knoxville, he looks kind of disappointed but nods. "I understand that. It's a big thing to take in all at once."

I nod and say, "It sure is." He looks kind of hurt that I wasn't making a bigger deal out of it, but didn't say anything else. After another minute or so he says, "So you're thinking about a new truck?"

I laugh. "Not a new one, maybe a little better than I've got right now."

We talk a little more about this and that and I say, "I ought to go feed Frankie. She's been awful good just to sit here and listen to us."

Melvin reaches out to Frankie and she gives his hand a lick. "She's a great dog, Boone. See you tomorrow, I hope."

I stand up and remember to fold up the map and put it in my back pocket. "Thanks for doing all this, Melvin."

"That was my pleasure, Boone. If you bring it back with you next time I'll just talk about one place, I promise."

I tell him I'd like to know more about New Orleans and he smiles and says, "I was only there for about a month and that was before Katrina, but it and Memphis would be my top two on the list of what I showed you today."

I don't know who Katrina was; maybe an old girlfriend or something, but I don't ask because I need to get going and if he gets started on something else I'll never get away.

I'm at the house feeding Frankie when the phone rings. I pick it up and say, "Hello."

"Well, you don't have to worry about your mother any more," says Aunt Claire.

As soon as I hear her voice I'm about half mad and half ashamed. I should have called Hannah back before this, just to see how she's doing, but I didn't. I guess it hasn't been that long since they were down here, and she never called me, but I'm the big brother and it's sort of my job to do that kind of stuff, I guess.

I don't remember anybody calling to check on me the last year or two, not until Claire needed me for something, so I'm not used to checking on people; nobody checks on me, so it doesn't come to mind. I want to ask Claire how Hannah's doing, but the way she started off has me all pissed off already and I'm not wanting to spend any more time on the phone with her than I have to.

She should have checked on me a long time ago, now that I think about it. I've been down here by myself for a while now, and nobody gave a big old damn one way or the other. She sure didn't; she could have been checking right along, and she didn't even pick up the phone. I hope she's been treating Hannah okay. She's just a little girl.

Neither one of us says anything for a minute. Frankie comes over and noses up to me; I take a quick look and her food bowl's almost empty already. I got to get to the store and get her some food. Finally Aunt Claire says something.

"Did you hear me, Boone? Are you still there? I said you don't have to worry about going to Memphis to get your momma anymore."

"You going to tell me what you're talking about?"

"Don't take that tone with me, young man. I'm your aunt, remember?"

"Yeah, I know who you are. Something happen to Momma?"

"Oh, nothing to speak of. Evidently Jake didn't stay gone for long; I got a call from her last night, she didn't even want to talk to Hannah, didn't ask about you, just said that she and Jake were probably moving out west somewhere, Phoenix, I think she said. I know she's my sister, but I just don't know what to think about her and men. I mean, your daddy was no prize, but I'll be switched if she didn't turn right around and hook up with somebody else that treats her like dirt. You'd think she'd have learned something, but I guess some people just can't learn from experience. I — "

264

I hang up the phone and say, "You want to go outside, Frankie?"

The phone starts ringing as I close the door. By the time we're halfway to the main building I can't hear it anymore.

I'm not going up to see Mark or Betty or anything like that, I'm just trying to get away from the phone. So I take Frankie all the way around the building and then back down to the house. I can hear the phone again when I get close to the house, but it stops before I get inside. Probably Claire again.

All this with Claire makes me want to talk to Hannah again, see if she's okay, but I don't want to get into it with Claire, so I decide to give it a few days before I call up there.

I look at Melvin's map a few times, at least once a day, and decide that if I can get a decent truck I'll probably go to one or two of these places. The trip he had laid out looks like it would take a month, and I don't know if I want to be gone that long. I remember him saying that Memphis and New Orleans were his top two from the trip he had laid out for me, so I might do them. I could do that and be back in a couple of weeks, I think. But that puts me to thinking about what I'd be coming back to if I do take off. I'll be taking Frankie with me, and there's nothing else here. Pretty much the only good memories are about

Nancy. And the bad memories, well, there's a bunch of them.

If Nancy is still going off to school then I might as well go on, see some stuff, and maybe come back here, maybe come back as far as Knoxville if that's where she is. And maybe not come back at all, I'm real torn up about this. I look over at Frankie; she's watching a bug crawl across the floor in the kitchen.

"So, Frankie, what do you think I ought to do? You want to go on a trip?"

She forgets all about the bug and comes over to me, ready to go.

"You want to stay here?"

She's just as excited when I say that, so Frankie is no help at all. That's part of the problem, I guess; I can't think of anybody to talk to about this. I know what Melvin will say, I've already talked to Mark, can't talk to Nancy, and Tiny's not going to say one way or the other. I'm feeling kind of stuck, but when I look around this place there's nothing here I care anything about. Course that's how I felt about my house too, except for Momma and Hannah. I did care about them. Still care about Hannah, but after what Claire told me on the phone about Momma and Jake, well, if I had ever thought about going to Memphis or wherever to get Momma and bring her home, that's gone now.

I guess part of that is I got no home to bring her to. This place doesn't count, and Claire's house doesn't count. As far as I know, we never went up there, so I don't know where it is exactly or what it looks like.

So, the places I've wanted to be, around here anyway, are the pool up above my old house, back in the woods, and Gamaliel's house while the old man was still around. After he left it was okay, nothing great, but better than that place I was living in with Momma and Daddy and Hannah. That's really about it. I think about Tiny; as far as I know, he's never lived anywhere but his folk's farm, but it's a really nice farm. I mean, the only place inside the house I've been is the kitchen. Tiny and I had pizza right out of the oven once when we had been up running the dogs and checking on the still. That still being gone is another reason I'm thinking that I might as well leave this place. I try to think about what I would need to do and what I would need to get to start it up again, and in a few minutes I'm thinking about something else. I can't keep it in my head. Tiny hasn't brought it up since the fire, so I'm thinking maybe that's not going to happen, him and me doing something. I guess when I run through what I've got that'll be the end of it. I get up and mix myself a drink with the regular stuff; don't have hardly any of the good stuff left, seems like. I hadn't really thought about what to do with my shine. Take it with me? If I got stopped they'd throw me in jail for sure, me being underage and carrying illegal liquor to boot.

It's the middle of the afternoon, and I'm sitting around drinking an S&S and feeling sorry for myself, and the phone rings. It's been a few days since Claire has tried to call me, so I pick up without thinking about it and say hello.

Chapter Thirty-Three

"Hey, Boone, it's me."

It's not Claire, but it takes me a second because Tiny almost never calls me.

"Hey, Tiny."

"You said something about a week or week and a half ago about wanting a truck. You still interested?"

I don't think it's been that long, but I say, "Yeah, I hadn't done any looking but I'm still interested. Why?"

"I got a friend looking for a new 4x4 truck, long bed, quad cab, you know, all the stuff you can get, and his wife Ruth has a truck she's had since before they got married. It's about 12 years old, but her brothers took real good care of it for her, and my friend is a pretty good mechanic too. I didn't think she'd ever let go of it, but he says she's made up her mind that they don't need two trucks. He says she's going to ask $5,000 for it, and I think that's pretty good. You won't be able to trade your old one in, she wouldn't have any use for it. You want to go take a look at it?"

"I don't know anything about buying and selling trucks, man. Reckon you could go with me and, you know, help me out a little?"

"I don't know, Boone, if you're talking about me loaning you some money, I don't have $5,000 just laying around."

It pisses me off a little that he would even say that. I didn't ask him for any damn money, and I start to tell him that, but he's still talking.

"But if you're talking about me coming along because I know something about cars and all that, sure, I'd be glad to."

I'm still working through being pissed off. I've been up there enough times to know that Tiny's family has all kinds of money. All those cars and trucks and four-wheelers and tools and barns and sheds and tractors, that house they live in, there's no way he doesn't have that kind of money. I mean, I'm not stupid. I didn't ask him for anything, he doesn't need to pretend he's poor or any of that shit.

"Boone? You still there?"

"Yeah. If you had the time, yeah, I'd sure take a look at it."

"My daddy always says never buy the first thing you look at, so we wouldn't be, you know, committed to anything just because we came up to look."

"Right. So where is this truck?"

Turns out the truck is about forty miles away and we can't go look at it until tomorrow afternoon, so I ask Tiny to go ahead and set it up. After I hang up I realize I didn't ask him anything about selling my truck.

Melvin is all excited when I see him just before lunch and tell him I might be buying a truck. He says, "So you might be able to go on the road after all. This is great news, Boone! I'm happy for you and a little envious at the same time."

He sure makes it sound good, this going on the road stuff. I'm able to get him talking about some of the places on his map, and he tells me enough about those places on the ocean and how great they are that I'm about to change my mind about starting with Memphis and New Orleans and go for Savannah and Charleston instead. He talks about going out on the ocean in a fishing boat far enough that you can't see land anywhere, and I don't know how I feel about that. Doesn't seem right somehow.

I meet up with Tiny in the afternoon the next day and ride with him up to his friend's house.

"Mac isn't home right now," Tiny says. "He works for one of the lumberyards and won't be back until after 4:00 or so. Ruth's here, though, and she's the one that drove the truck most, so she can tell you what it's like. They just had a baby, so she might be kind of busy, but she said we could come up and take a look, drive it if we wanted to."

The truck is a lot better than the one I've got. It's got plenty of room in the back of the cab, back behind the seat, for Frankie to ride if she wanted to. There's a couple of little seats back there, look like kids' seats.

It's got a V-8 engine, and Tiny says it runs great. It feels bigger than my truck when I sit behind the wheel. Ruth is bouncing the baby up and down and finally says, "She's hungry. I need to go inside and feed her. You guys want to drive it? I'll be fifteen or twenty minutes anyway, she's kind of a slow eater, so you can take it out and I'll be done by the time you get back."

Tiny tosses me the keys and climbs in the passenger door. "Now it's not that little toy car the preacher's got, Boone. Don't go at the curves the way you say you can with that thing; you'll put this truck in the ditch if you do. It's got a lot more power than your truck, too, so watch out for that."

I'm about to tell him that I know how to drive and he needs to just shut up and sit there, but I'm thinking maybe I better listen, they're his friends, and I don't know anything about this truck.

By the time we get back to Ruth's house I'm ready to buy the thing, and Tiny is trying to slow me down.

"You know this is the first one we've looked at, Boone. The only thing you've got to compare this to is your old truck, so you know it's going to look good."

I know all this, but the thought of getting back in my old piece of shit truck after driving this one makes me sick to my stomach.

A couple of days later we go to a car lot that Tiny knows about, and they've got three trucks that are about $5,000. One of them is a Toyota, it's smaller than the other two and I don't even want to drive it, but Tiny says if we're going to do this right we need to check it out.

The salesman is a pushy little bastard, and that makes me not want to buy from him just because I don't like him much. He follows us all over the car lot, running his mouth, until I finally turn to Tiny and say, "Let's get out of here before I lose my shit and punch this guy right in the face."

Tiny's laughing when we pull out on the highway. "You can't let that kind of thing bother you, Boone. All car salesmen are like that. It's just what they do." He looks over at me. "You know you never did drive that Toyota."

"I don't care, Tiny, that guy just pissed me off. If that's what they're all like I don't want to go to any more car lots. I'd just as soon buy from some guy that just wants to get rid of his truck. I mean, that's how I'll end up selling mine."

After he gets me back to my truck I go by the bank and it's closed; I don't usually pay attention to what day it is and it takes me a minute to remember it's Sunday. It's not until Tuesday that I get back to the bank and pull out $6,000 from the box. I feel like I ought to be thanking Gamaliel for this, but that feels kind of weird, so I just put it and my truck title in my pocket and go on home. I put $1,000 in the kitchen drawer with the title and keep the rest in my pocket.

Wednesday morning I call Tiny and say, "Let's go back up to Ruth's and buy that truck."

He tries to talk me into looking around some more but I'm pretty much over it, I just want that truck. I wish I'd bought it when we first went up there, but I didn't, I did what Tiny said I'm supposed to do. I looked at other trucks.

On the way up there I take the $5,000 out of my pocket and put it next to Tiny on the seat. "You know all about how to do this kind of thing. Okay if I just watch, try to learn how it's done?"

He's looking at the road, but when he glances down and sees the money, he almost runs into the guy ahead of us. It's a Chevy, I can tell by the emblem on the rear end, but that's all I know about it except that he was trying to turn off and we damn near climbed right up his tailpipe.

"Where the hell did that come from?"

"I brought it with me. I figured we might need it if they haven't already sold the truck."

I point at the road. "You ought to be watching the road, man."

"I'm watching the damn road, and I know you brought it with you. Where did you get that kind of money, man?"

He sounds like he thinks I might have stolen it.

"You know you're kind of sounding like you think I might've stole this money. I didn't, but if that's what you think, you can just pull over right now. I won't ride with a man that thinks I'm a thief."

He slows down and I'm about ready to pull the handle and bail out of the truck when I look up and see we're coming up on a red light.

"I don't think you're a thief, Boone, don't go flying off on me. You say you didn't steal it and that's the end of it. I got no reason to doubt you. You got to admit it's a little surprising."

I'm breathing pretty hard and trying to settle down, so it takes me a second to answer. "Yeah, I can see that."

Neither one of us says anything for a while and then he says, "So, you want me to get it for less if I can?"

I nod, then realize he's watching the road, not looking at me. "Yeah, if you can. I'd appreciate it."

"I'll try, but you know they've got that new kid and all . . . ."

Now I feel bad about trying to get the truck for less money.

"Look, Tiny, just do what you think's right, okay?"

He nods and we go back to being quiet.

We're getting close to Ruth and Mac's house when I say, "Gamaliel gave it to me, okay?"

Tiny doesn't say anything for a minute and then says, "You know, that makes all kinds of sense to me. I know you two were tight, and I can see him doing that for you."

"Right now you and Nancy are the only people that know about it, so if you could just keep it quiet, I'd appreciate it."

"Hey, it's not my business, man. I won't mention it to anybody, but if Nancy brings it up, I don't know that I can act like I'm surprised or anything."

Ruth is standing out in the yard when we pull in and Tiny says, "I called her and let her know we were on our way."

We get out and she says, "You guys want some lunch?"

"No, thanks," says Tiny. "We're fine."

I'm pretty hungry, but I let it go.

"I talked to Mac and he told me to go ahead and do what I think is best. Said it's my truck and I don't need him to come home just for this."

I try to imagine Daddy saying that to Momma and I just can't.

So she and Tiny start talking and they're not talking about the truck. It's all about people they know, and when was the last time you saw so-and-so, and how's the baby doing, and does Mac still like the job, and just about the time I think Tiny might have forgotten why we came up here, he says, "So Mac's going to get himself a new truck."

Chapter Thirty-Four

"That's right," Ruth says. "He's all on fire about it, too. Can't stop talking about it, waiting on it to get here."

"Damn, Ruth, did he order one special?"

She shakes her head. "No, nothing like that. He wanted one of those charcoal grey ones and the dealer down in Chattanooga has one and I guess the dealers swap inventory all the time. Anyway, he's waiting on it, supposed to be here day after tomorrow."

"You going to sneak out after he gets it home, put the first scratch on it and get that out of the way? You know how he'll be, worse than with that baby, until it gets broke in good."

Ruth laughs, and she and Tiny spend a couple of minutes talking about Mac and then Tiny says, "So you two decided you don't want two trucks in the yard?"

I almost miss it, but that's when it turns into a serious talk. They go back an forth about the price, the condition of the truck, and then they're talking about the new baby and how they're fixing up the place, and then back to bargaining. Tiny doesn't act like he's in any hurry, almost like he's not interested, and Ruth is kind of back and forth about whether or not she wants to get rid of it at all, and the only time it's not smooth and easy is when Tiny tells her that it's me that wants the truck. She cuts her eyes over at me and then back to Tiny. "He can't talk for himself?" She looks at me again and now it's kind of unfriendly, but more like suspicious, like she doesn't trust me.

I start to say something and Tiny jumps in. "We were talking on the way up here and I told him that since I've known you guys forever that, if he didn't mind, I'd do most of the talking. Boone's okay, he just doesn't talk much."

"That right?" She's still looking at me.

"Yeah, Tiny's right. People give me a hard time about it all the time. It's a nice truck though, and the one I've got's a real piece of, uh, junk."

She grins at that and says, "Sure it's not a piece of shit?"

I can't help it, I laugh out loud. "You might be right about that."

Then it's all okay again, and I try to be part of the back and forth, but still it's mostly Tiny, and he talks her down to $4,300. "I'll go get the title," she says, and heads toward the house.

Tiny turns to me. "Okay?"

"Yeah, thanks, man."

"Now if she doesn't fill in the sales price on the title, you'll have to put it in yourself. You have to pay taxes on whatever you put in there."

"So what should I put down?"

"I'd probably put $3,000," he says. "No sense giving the government more than you have to."

Sure enough, she leaves that part blank and hands me a pen to sign my name. Tiny nods and I fill in the amount we talked about and sign my name.

"Here's the keys," Ruth says. She doesn't even look at the title, probably doesn't want to know what I put down.

"Thanks," I say, and stick out my hand. "You got a real nice place here."

"I'll see you back at my place," says Tiny. and that's where I go, trying to get used to the new truck.

I think about offering Tiny some money for doing all the work, but I know how I'd feel if somebody did that to me after I did them a favor, so I don't bring it up. I drive the new truck down to the old folk's home and Tiny follows me, then takes me back to his place to pick up my old truck.

"Thanks again, man," I say. "If you run across a camper top that'd fit the new one, let me know. I think I'd like to have one."

Mark says it looks like a good truck. "Better than the one you've been driving, no question about that," he says with a grin. Betty says I need to get rid of my old truck as soon as I can, so I don't take up two parking spaces. At first I think she's just playing with me, since the lot's never full here, but she looks serious and I tell her I'll sell it as soon as I can. Mark says I should park it so the windshield faces the road and put a "For Sale" sign propped up so anybody that drives by can see it, so that's what I do.

I think Melvin's more excited than anybody, even though he says I should have bought something that gets better gas mileage. "You can go anywhere in that thing," he says when he sees it. "All you need is a camper top and a sleeping bag for when you stop for the night, and you're good to go. The whole country is yours to explore!"

The only person that doesn't know about the truck is Nancy, and it's been over a week since I talked to her. I'm about half scared to try her house again and sounds like her dad's got her cell phone, so I can't really try that way. I think she would've called me if she could, so that makes me even more worried.

There's not much in the kitchen to eat, so I take a little bit of that $700 that Tiny saved me on the truck and head for the grocery store. I need frozen stuff, especially that meat lover's pizza I got the last time, and macaroni and Thunderstorm and it's about time for the good tomatoes to hit the stores, so I'm planning a pretty big trip.

I'm coming out of the first aisle when I see Nancy and her mom two aisles down with a half full cart heading for the milk and cheese section. I forget about all the stuff I was going to get and get up right behind them.

"Hey, Nancy."

She starts to turn around and her mom grabs her arm and pulls her along and now they're moving really fast, like they're trying to get away from me. I try again.

"Hey, Nancy, it's me, Boone. Hold up a second."

Nancy's mom says something to her, real quiet, and Nancy keeps going and her mom turns to face me.

"You need to leave us alone," she says, trying to keep her voice quiet.

"What?"

"I said you need to leave us alone," she's still talking low, but I'm closer now and I can see fear in her eyes, like I used to see in Momma's.

"Let me talk to Nancy," I say, and I start to push my cart past her. She grabs hold of it and pushes it back toward me.

282

"You go on back to the other side of the store, right now!" She lets go with one more push and hurries around the corner. I'm right behind her. My cart is back in the middle of the aisle.

I come around the corner and Nancy is standing there. I start to reach for her and she backs up. "If my Dad saw you come into the store . . . . I can't talk to you, Boone, I can't!"

"Is this about — "

I stop when I see the look on her face. She's staring past me down toward the front of the store. I turn around and Stan is walking toward us, walking fast.

"Hi, Stan," I say. "How's it going?"

He goes right past me and is right up in Nancy's face. "Did you call him? Did you and your mother make up this trip to the store so you could sneak off with that piece of trash?"

She's shaking her head and saying, "No, no," over and over and I'm so mad I can't even think. I grab his arm from behind and I guess he wasn't expecting that because I spin him around toward me and he kind of loses his balance for a second. He gets it back quick, though, and steps right up to me.

"You stay away from my little girl, you hear me?"

People are turning to look, he's really loud, and I say, "I don't know what your problem is, Stan, but you might step back just a bit." I can feel my heart pounding and I know I'm red as a beet. My fists are clenched and I'm about ready to swing on him. I say, "I came up to say hi, and that's what I'm going to do," and I start to step around him. He puts out an arm to block me, I push it down, and he brings it right back up and grabs the front of my shirt. I can smell the beer on him. He's had more than a few.

By now Nancy and her mom are both screaming at Stan and I'm getting ready to punch him in the gut and somebody takes hold of me from behind. Whoever it is hauls me back away from Stan and he starts to follow, but Nancy and her mom grab him and hold on.

"Settle down, now, come on, settle down." Somebody is right in my ear.

I'm twisting around and trying to get away and eventually I get turned around so I can see who it is. It's not anybody I recognize. He's a little taller than me, and he might be a couple of years older, but he doesn't look familiar.

"Who the hell are you?"

"I'm the shift manager. Name's Eric. You want to come with me over this way?"

I look back and Stan is staring at me. Nancy is still holding his arm and she won't look at me at all. She's staring at the floor and then she looks up at Stan and says, "Come on, Dad, let's finish up here and go home."

He looks at her and it's a second or two before he says, "Okay, let's find your mother." He and Nancy go around the corner and disappear.

"Is this your cart over here?" Eric isn't pulling me along, but he is leading the way. I follow along without thinking about it much. We stop at the cart and I look down into it. There are four Thunderstorms and some macaroni and three or four cans of soup. I hadn't gotten to the cheese and ice cream yet.

"What's your name?"

"Boone. What the hell was that all about?"

"Funny," says Eric, "I was just getting ready to ask you that same thing."

So I tell him that Nancy's my girl and I was just going up to talk to her and her dad came up and started in on me. I don't tell him the rest, about the pills and how I think Stan thinks I'm screwing his little girl.

"Listen, why don't you go back to the other end of the store and make sure you didn't miss anything. By the time you get to where we are right now they'll probably be gone and you can finish your shopping. This is not the place to have it out with her dad, you understand?"

It's hard for me to be mad at Eric, he's being so reasonable about the whole thing, so I nod and say, "Sounds like a plan."

"Good," he says, and holds up his fist and for a second I don't know what to do and then I remember from some TV show and I put my fist up and bump it against his. "You take care, Boone."

It takes me a little bit to go all the way through the store and when I come out the parking lot is almost empty. I climb into my truck and head back home, trying to figure out what happened.

The more I think about it the more it makes sense that Stan found out about the birth control pills and isn't letting Nancy out of his sight. When he saw me he figured I was why she had the pills and he came after me. I could see him getting all bent out of shape about that. I mean, his little girl and all.

Him calling me trash, though, that was, well, if I had come from a family with a nice house and a nice car or two and lots of money, he wouldn't have gone after me in the store like that. And he sure as hell wouldn't have called me trash.

Well, the hell with him. The hell with the whole damn family.

Chapter Thirty-Five

About an hour after I get home and get the groceries put up somebody knocks on the door.

I've got a half empty S&S in my hand and I'm watching a really stupid cop show on TV and I don't feel like answering the door or the phone or talking to anybody about anything.

As a matter of fact, I'm ready to get in the truck right now with Frankie and my shotgun and money and Melvin's map and just start driving.

That gets me started thinking about what I will put in the truck. I can't really do anything until I get a camper top, but when I do I'll be ready to figure out what I'm going to do.

Whoever's at the door knocks again, and then Betty says, "Boone? Are you in there? Mr. Stannard is asking for you. Can you come up to my office? Boone?"

I'm not in the mood to talk to anybody, and it takes me a second to remember who she's talking about.

"I'll be up there in a minute!" I shout at the door. Wonder what Melvin wants with me that couldn't wait til tomorrow?

"Come as soon as you can," she says. "He says it's important."

I wait for a minute and then look out the window. Betty is halfway back to the main building. Going to the kitchen, I finish off the S&S and tell Frankie, "You want to go see Melvin?"

Frankie is always up for going anywhere anytime. She's at the front door before I can get out of the kitchen. I grab her leash and we head up to Betty's office.

Melvin is there with her and some guy I've seen before. It takes me a minute to remember that he's Melvin's son-in-law; I only met him one other time. He stands up and puts out his hand and I shake it, then he sits back down next to Melvin.

"You remember Stuart, Boone? He's my son-in-law."

"I remember, Melvin. How are you, Stuart?"

Stuart says he's fine, and then we just sit there staring at each other for a minute or two and then Stuart says, "I understand you have a truck for sale."

That was not what I thought this was going to be about. I'd been thinking on the way up to Betty's office, is Melvin sick, is he moving, did I say something to piss him off, but I never thought Stuart might be here in town, and I'm wondering what he wants with my old piece of shit truck.

I just nod and Stuart goes on, "I have been thinking about getting a truck, just for occasional use, you know, hauling trash and picking up shrubs for the yard, that sort of thing."

While he's talking I'm trying to remember where he's from and I can't do it.

He says, "I understand it's not a new vehicle, but I don't need anything fancy, and I was wondering if you'd be willing to let it go for, say, $500 — " Melvin pokes at him and he says, "I meant to say, $1,000?"

This is more charity. I know just what's going on here, and I don't like it. I'm about ready to tell them all to shove it and go back down to the house when Betty says, "I sure wish you'd take him up on this, Boone, you know we talked about you taking up two parking spaces and how you'd eventually have to do something about that."

Melvin jumps in. "I already told Stuart that it's only good for a run to the dump or the landscapers once in a while, and he's okay with that. He was all ready to spend a lot more and get more truck than he needed when I told him about you."

One thing is, this is just about my last tie to Daddy. When I get rid of this truck, there won't be much of anything left of him in my life. I would've thought that would be fine with me, but staring it in the face like I am right now, I don't know, I just don't know.

Then I start thinking about sitting in the living room of that old house or being out in the back yard and hearing that thing top the hill and all of us, Momma, Hannah, and me, waiting to hear how he turned off the road and came into the yard and how hard he slammed the door getting out of the truck so we'd know whether to hide or not. I think about that time he backed me up to the rear end of the truck and the tailgate was down and hit me in the back of the legs and I fell backwards and hit my head hard enough to raise a knot and how he laughed til he started coughing. I think about the time he was driving and mad as hell at somebody or other and put it into the ditch and jerked it right back out again just before we got to one of those narrow bridges with the concrete rails on each side.

I can't really think of any good memories that have anything to do with that old piece of shit.

"Tell you what," I say, and Melvin and Betty are looking at me and Stuart is looking at Melvin, "I don't really need two trucks and I bet I can get a camper for the one I just bought and maybe have some left over from that thousand. So it's yours if you want it."

Stuart nods and for some reason Melvin looks disappointed. He's shaking his head and then he stops and says, "Okay, Stu, looks like you've got a truck. Boone, would you go get the title so we can make this official?"

I stand up and so does Frankie. We go down to the house and get the title out of the drawer and take it back to Betty's office. When I get back Stuart is gone and Melvin says, "Sorry, Boone, but Stu had to step out to take a phone call. He left me the check, though, so if you'd just sign over the title he can fill in his information."

The title looks like the one for my new truck, so I know where I'm supposed to sign it. The thing is still in Daddy's name, so I scribble something that looks like Nathaniel Hammond and hand it to Melvin. He doesn't even look at it, just folds it up and puts it in his pocket and says to Betty, "Would you give us just a minute?"

Betty closes the door behind her and Melvin says, "Okay, Boone, you said yes to that way too quickly. I know Stu, and you could have probably gotten at least three, maybe four hundred more out of him. Next time you're in this kind of position don't be too anxious to get it over with."

"Now don't get mad," he says, holding up one hand. He can see my face getting red, and Frankie is up on her feet. "I'm just saying you're new at this. Next time you'll get a better deal, I'm sure of it."

"You got the check?" I just want to get out of here.

He sighs. "I do." He digs in the other pocket of his jacket and pulls it out. He hands it to me and says, "If you want to talk more about the places I have suggested on that map, you let me know. Would you tell Betty to come on back in when you leave? I can tell you really want to get back to your house, and I'm a little tired."

Betty is in the hallway talking to Stuart and I tell her that Melvin wants to go take a nap or something. Stuart steps over to me and holds his hand out. "Melvin says you might be going on a trip. Have a good, safe journey."

I shake his hand and try not to look at Betty. I don't think I've said anything to her about this, since until I saw Nancy at the store I wasn't even planning to go anywhere.

"Well," I say, "I wasn't going to go anytime soon, but thanks."

He and Betty go back into her office and Frankie and I go on back to the house. I put the check with the other money and start thinking about making something to eat. It's dusky dark outside and I'm feeling hungry, and I have lots of food now.

"What do you think, Frankie? Sandwich or pizza?"

The next day I'm up by nine and decide to make the rounds with Frankie before lunch; it's a pretty day, so lots of people are out walking or sitting, and Frankie is glad to see all of them. I save Melvin til last, as usual.

He's reading a book and waves me over.

"This is a traveler's guide to the Southeast," he says, and hands the book to me. It's really small, one of those paperbacks you can put in your back pocket.

"I don't know, Melvin, I'm not much of a reader."

"It's a very useful book, Boone, You should take it with you when you leave on your trip. It's the kind of book that you can just read a few pages, get some information about where you're going, and put it down until you need it again."

I stick it in my pocket and Melvin starts talking about New Orleans again, and how the drive over Lake Ponche-something is such a great way to come up on the city, and how the French Quarter is a great place but the city gets real dangerous if you go more than a few blocks away from the Quarter, and how he had one of the best meals he'd ever eaten in a little out-of-the-way restaurant that didn't look like anything from the outside, and listening to him I'm starting to think I ought to go get a camper top and load up right away.

There's the sound of a big diesel engine from out in the parking lot and I stand up to go see what's going on. Melvin says, "Sit back down, Boone, I'm just getting to the good part."

"I'll be right back," I say, and Frankie and I turn the corner in time to see a guy hooking my old truck up to a set of chains and hauling it up onto a flatbed truck. The truck says DeeCee Salvage on the side, and the guy, he looks like he's half again as big as Tiny, throws some straps across the truck and cranks them down tight and climbs back up into the cab and takes off.

When I get back to where Melvin was sitting he's gone, and I look around and so is everybody else. Must be lunchtime, so I go back down to the house and check Frankie's food and water. "I'm going out for a drive, girl," I say. "You stay here and I'll be back real soon."

I grab the check from Stuart and $200 from the cash I've got in the drawer and go to the bank. I put it all in my checking account, which I almost never use, but if I'm going to buy a camper top I might need to. I'm halfway out the door before I remember about the other time I put a check in the bank and they told me I had to wait for three days or some shit like that. I go back in and ask, and sure enough, there's a three day wait. I try to think how much I've got back at the house and figure that if I find something before the time's up I'll either pay for it out of what I've got at home or run back by the safety deposit box and get some more. I decide while I'm out to go get a burger at the volcano place. I"m still wondering about the DeeCee Salvage truck and what that's all about, but I can't do anything about that til I see Melvin again.

I don't end up getting a burger at the volcano place. They're running a special on something called a Buffalo Chicken Wing platter and I decide to give that a try. Sandy's working again, and I end up at one of her tables.

"Hello, Boone. Too bad about Nancy, huh?"

I'm all ready to order this chicken platter, but her asking that stops me cold.

"What about Nancy?"

Sandy looks at me a little funny and says, "I can't believe she didn't tell you."

Chapter Thirty-Six

"Didn't tell me what?"

Sandy looks around at the rest of the place. It's about half full and there's two or three people getting ready to come in, so she says, "I can't talk right now, Boone, it's getting busy in here."

"Well why don't you just stand here for a second while I look at this menu one more time and you talk while I'm looking," I say. I'm trying real hard not to shout or anything, but it's hard, because I saw Nancy just yesterday, and I know something's bad wrong. "You can tell me about this Buffalo chicken thing. And while you're at it, you can't believe Nancy didn't tell me what?"

"You'd really like the Buffalo chicken wings, Boone, if you like spicy food. They've got a real kick to them, and we've got the best around. You want me to bring you some out?"

"While you're waiting on me to say yes, tell me what's going on," I say, and I can tell my voice is getting a little loud. Sandy looks around again and says, "You got to keep your voice down, Boone."

I nod and she says, "She came in here earlier today and both her mom and dad were with her, and her dad was talking to her real low, but I heard just a little bit when I came up to take their order. He said if she thought those pills meant she could just jump — "

She stops and I say, "What the hell does that mean, Sandy?" But I think I was right about what's going on.

"He stopped because that's when I came up to the table and he saw me coming and shut up. You want fries with those wings?"

"What?"

"You get one side, most people want fries. You want fries?"

"Sure, and a Thunderstorm."

"We don't carry Thunderstorm. Sorry."

I look around to see what's on the other tables. "You got sweet tea?"

She smiles. "So sweet it'll make your teeth hurt."

"Okay, then. I'll take some sweet tea."

She writes it all down, even though there's not that much to the order, and goes off to the kitchen. I sit back and think about what she said, and it sure sounds like her dad found out about the birth control pills. It kind of makes sense that he came running when he saw me in the grocery store talking to Nancy, so I can't really fault him for that.

He didn't need to call me trash, though.

Sandy comes back with a big glass of tea and a straw.

"I don't need a straw," I say. "Give that thing to somebody else."

She sticks it back in her apron and says, "That's all I really know, Boone, but he sure was mad. Wouldn't let her out of his sight except when she went to the bathroom. I started to go in there after her so maybe I could find out something, but her mom was right behind her. Your wings will be out in just a bit. Enjoy your tea."

She's right about the tea. It's almost too sweet for me, and I like mine pretty heavy on the sugar. I get it about half drunk by the time she's out with a plate of chicken wings and little tiny chicken legs, and they're covered in some kind of orange sauce. There are two little bowls of white stuff and a pile of french fries.

"Can I get you anything else? Oh, I almost forgot. You'll need these," and she pulls out a handful of napkins and sets them on the table. "This is a really messy meal. I'll go get you some more tea in just a second."

I pick up a wing and take a bite. She wasn't joking about the spice. I grab the tea without wiping my hands with a napkin and damn near drop the glass.

Turns out one of the little bowls has ranch dressing and the other one has a few chunks of something in it. I dip the next wing in the chunky stuff and it's really good. Sandy is back with the tea pitcher and asks me how it is and I can't answer because my mouth is full. She laughs and says, "Told you," and fills up my tea.

I'm just about finished and she comes back by. I say, "There's a couple of dollars under the salt shaker on that table over there."

She looks and says, "That's not my table, that's Franci's. Looks like a pretty small tip for how many people were at that table. She was back and forth six or eight times taking care of them."

So that's extra money for the waitress. I decide to leave Sandy some money, too, since she told me what was going on with Nancy.

On the way back home I'm thinking about the last thing Sandy said to me.

"Next time I see Nancy I'll try to let her know you were asking about her. Does she have your cell number?"

When I told her I didn't have a cell number she looked at me like I had three eyes or something. "Are you serious? Everybody's got a cell phone, Boone! I can't believe you don't have one!" She just went on and on about it and I was about ready to pick up that money I was going to leave her and decided not to, but she kind of pissed me off.

By the time I get back to the house I've figured out that she's right. If I'm really going on this trip I might need to call somebody or somebody might need to call me. I guess I ought to get a phone. Maybe Mark can help me do that, since I don't know anything about how much they cost or anything.

When I find out that you can spend hundreds of dollars on a phone I'm about to forget the whole thing, and Mark says, "You can get what they call a pre-paid phone, they're cheap, but they don't have all the stuff that the nice ones do."

I tell him I don't care about all the stuff. He takes me to Wal-Mart and shows me what they've got, and I tell him just pick something out, that I don't care. He gets me a phone and some kind of card that he says is good for three months as long as I don't talk more than an hour.

Mark shows me how to charge up the phone and get the 90 days started, and I call his office to make sure that everything works.

Now I've got a cell phone. Probably was going to have to get one anyway before the trip.

Chapter Thirty-Seven

A couple of days later I'm up at Tiny's, helping him out with a widow-maker in a stand of trees just back of their house. It takes almost an hour to get it to the ground, Tiny on one of the tractors jerking it sideways, until the last big branch lets go and the tree comes all the way down.

"Boy, that's a mother of a tree," he says while we're coiling up the ropes and getting everything put back in the shed. "Probably start cutting it up for firewood next week. If you're interested in a little exercise, come on up. Mom'll feed you and we might find time to take a break or two ourselves."

"It depends on whether I'm still in town," I say, and he stops halfway to the shed, a big coil of rope hanging off his shoulder.

"Where are you going?"

I shrug. "I don't know. Hell, I might not go, but this guy Melvin at the home, he's been pushing me to get out of town, see some new places, even got a road map and told me where I ought to go to start with."

"That actually sounds like fun," he hangs the rope on the wall and turns around to go get the next coil. "How long would you be gone? I mean, when would you think you might be back?"

Until he says that, I had been kind of back and forth about it. Now I say it out loud for maybe the first time.

"What would be the use in coming back here?"

He sits down on the tailgate of his truck and just stares at me.

"I mean," I say, about half talking to Tiny and half to myself, "I'd need a camper top for sure, and I ought to make a list of things to take, you know, some kind of cushion to sleep on, maybe a cooler to keep stuff cold, I don't know. Hadn't really thought too much about that part."

Tiny's still staring at me, and I don't say anything else. After a minute he says, "Hell, Boone, I could get you a camper top tomorrow, if you're willing to take a used one. I got a friend over at DeeCee Salvage, they've got hundreds of old junk cars, I bet they've got two dozen trucks with the front end smashed all to hell and nothing wrong with the rear. I'd bet some of them have campers.

"That part's easy. You really thinking about gettin out? Like, for good? What about . . ." and he gets this look on his face and after a second he says, "You know, I guess there's not a lot holding you here, is there?"

I shake my head.

He grins at me. "Boy, that's tempting. I mean, the thought of just hopping in the truck and getting on the road and, you know, driving until something looked interesting." He looks at his house and then back at me. "You wouldn't be interested in some company, would you? I mean, just for the first part."

"That would depend on who it was," I say, and now I'm grinning, too, and the more I think about it the more it seems like the right thing to do, getting away from here.

"I'll give that some thought," he says. "Want me to call about that camper top, maybe go up tomorrow and look at what they've got, if they have anything?"

"Sure."

Turns out only two of the trucks have camper tops and neither one fits, but the guy Tiny talks to up there makes a couple of calls and tells Tiny there's one in Greeneville that's the right size. We go up there in my truck and it's a small salvage yard, but the camper looks okay, and even though I'm still no good at this haggling thing, I get him to knock thirty dollars off the price if Tiny and I get it off the old truck and onto mine.

"That was good," Tiny says on the way back.

"What are you talking about?"

"In a place like that you always have to get the part yourself. When you offered, though, it gave him an excuse to drop the price a little. See, people don't want to give in for no reason. So you give them a reason to work with you, and sometimes they will."

"Oh."

That night I sit down on the couch and start thinking seriously about what it would take to get ready to leave. There's just a few things:

> Something to sleep on and a couple of boxes to store stuff in
> Decide something about the guns, Daddy's shotgun and Gamaliel's old rifle
> What to do with the money in the bank
> What to do about Nancy
> Tell Hannah and Aunt Claire
> Tell Mark and Betty
> What to do with the shine I've still got
> Stuff for Frankie, food and food dish, water dish
> Find out if Tiny's going or not
> Talk to Melvin

I feel like there's more but I'll be damned if I can think what it might be. I guess there's not much keeping me here if that's all the list I can make. I decide that tomorrow's soon enough to start working on all this and get out Melvin's map. If I'm going to do this I guess I ought to learn how to read one of these things. Most of what I'm looking at doesn't make any sense.

He's got some places circled and a couple have circles and arrows pointing to them. Memphis he talks about almost every time I see him, so I know about that one and New Orleans, too. There are a few places I'm going to need to ask him about, though. He's never talked about Biloxi, or Destin, or something called Okefenokee, or Edisto, or Saint Augustine. Hell, I'm looking at this map and I don't even know which direction to head first.

I definitely need to talk to Melvin again before I hit the road.

I'm trying to figure out how to get hold of Nancy so I can give her this cell number I have now, because it's pretty sure that I'm going on this trip, and I don't know where exactly I'm going or how long I'll be in any one place.

Trouble is, I don't know any of Nancy's friends.

It takes me a little while to realize that there's something wrong with that. Maybe she was ashamed of me and didn't want any of her friends to know that she was hanging around me. Maybe deep down she thinks I'm trash, just like Stan does. The more I think about this the more it seems like that must be exactly what's going on here. She never cared anything about me.

"Boone, you know that's not true."

I've just finished telling Mark all the stuff I have been thinking about Nancy, and when I run out of stuff to say he shakes his head and says I'm wrong.

"How would you know that?"

"I've seen you two together, Boone. It doesn't take a genius or some kind of specialist to recognize love when it's as strong as it is between you two. I promise you she wasn't playing with you and I guarantee she does not think you are trash."

I don't know about all that, but I really want to believe him.

"So you're going to take Melvin's advice? I think that's great. Any idea how long you'll be gone?"

Mark and I have been talking off and on about this ever since I told him about the map and Melvin's ideas about me seeing the world, or at least a little bit of it. I haven't told him I'm not coming back at all.

"No, I really don't know how long. A while, I guess."

Well, I've got your number, Boone, so I might give you a call now and then. If that's all right with you."

I nod.

"Don't give up on Nancy just because her dad's being really protective right now. You know he is trying to come to terms with the fact that his little girl is growing up, moving out of the house, going out on her own. You might be a little young to appreciate what that feels like to a parent."

I just look at him until I can see that he's remembering about my parents.

"I'm sorry, Boone, that was poorly stated on my part." He looks like somebody that just realized they said the worst thing they could have said, and it's their job to say the best thing.

"Yeah, well, you're right. I don't have any idea what that's like, Mark."

Now he looks like I slapped him across the face.

He's quiet for a minute or two and then he says, "You want me to try to get a message to her?"

I stand up. "I'll think about that. Listen, Mark, I got to go. I'll see you later on."

He's on his feet, too. "I'd like that, Boone, and, again, I'm sorry I misspoke."

I'm about halfway out the door and he says, "Maybe you can take me for a drive in your new truck. How about lunch tomorrow?"

I say okay and leave out the side door. I don't want to run into Betty.

The next morning I go to Wal-Mart. We never went when I was a kid, you got to have at least a little money or it's a big waste of time. There's things I need to buy, so I go in and get one of those buggys

307

and head for the part of the store that sells camping stuff. I figure that's a good place to start.

Man, they've got everything in the world here. I could spend a thousand dollars easy, but I only brought a couple of hundred. That's probably a good thing. They have air mattresses to sleep on, and sleeping bags to get inside when it's cold, and boxes to store stuff in, and all kinds of other shit. I wouldn't have room to get into the back of the truck if I bought everything I thought I might need.

I know they've got Wal-Marts all over the place, so I get some boxes and a sleeping bag and an air mattress and a dog bed for Frankie. The chances are good I'll be making another run before I leave town, but I got to say it feels pretty good to get started doing this.

When I think about it, I've been just sitting on my ass for a while now. The time I spent watching Gamaliel's house I didn't have to do anything besides be there, and it got me out of our old place but that was about it. This thing at the old folks home is more Betty and Carrie feeling sorry for me than anything else, and I sort of knew that but I let it happen anyway. And what I've had going with Nancy, Mark called it love, and I don't know about that, but it sure was nice having somebody care that much about me. I'm kind of afraid that Stan's going to put a stop to that, though, however Nancy might feel. She's eighteen and all, but it's not like she's got money of her own.

I barely see the stop sign in time to stop, and all the stuff I just bought slams up against the front of the truck bed. I need to pay attention to driving this thing or I'll wreck it and then be putting off this trip for however long it takes to get it running again.

After I pull into the parking lot I sit in the truck for a little while before I go get Mark. I'm thinking I might need his help with some of this preparation stuff, especially with Hannah and Nancy. I can't get hold of Nancy because of Stan and I don't want to call Hannah because I might end up talking to Aunt Claire.

I can talk to Mark about all this at lunch.

Chapter Thirty-Eight

Seems like I'm spending a lot of time in this same restaurant. Mark and I go in and Sandy is on again today, and we end up in her area.

"Hello, Boone, long time no see," she says. "And who do we have here?"

Her voice sounds a little different, and when I look at her she's not smiling, She's just looking at Mark.

"Hi," he says, "I'm Mark, I'm a friend of Boone's."

"Well," she says, "any friend of Boone's. You two want menus?"

She brings them and hurries off even though the place is not that busy. I look at Mark and he's studying the menu like nothing happened.

"What was that about?" I say.

"What?" he asks. "Oh, you mean Sandy? Don't worry about it, Boone, I'm used to it." He goes back to looking at the menu.

It's been a long time since I thought about Mark being a black guy, but I'm guessing that's what this is all about.

"Hey, man, we can go somewhere else if you want to."

He shrugs. "Can't run away from it, now, can I? It's okay, Boone, really it is."

"I don't know, Mark, I don't like it much when people treat me like I'm white trash."

He gives me a look I can't figure out and says, "It's not exactly the same thing, but I do appreciate that you kind of understand. Thanks. Now, what should I order here?"

I tell him about the Buffalo wings and he shakes his head. "Too messy for me today, I've got things to do this afternoon and can't have orange sauce on the front of my shirt. How about the fish sandwich?"

"Never had it. The stuff I've had here is good, though."

He decides to try it and we order and after Sandy leaves I say, "There's some stuff I need you to help me with, if you're willing. First, I'd like to let Hannah know I'm going on this trip and make sure she's okay, but the last time I talked to Claire she was badmouthing Momma and I won't listen to that shit again. Reckon you could get her a letter or something if I gave it to you?"

He nods. "I can do that."

Something else that I just now think of and before I can give it any thought I just say it. "And I've got some money that I'd really like Hannah to have, but I figure if Claire gets her hands on it Hannah won't see any of it."

Sandy brings us our food and we take a few bites. "This fish is pretty good," Mark says, "not the best I've ever had, but good. So, how much money are we talking about?"

I say the first thing that pops into my head. "I don't know, I guess about two thousand."

Mark has his sandwich in his hands and puts it right back down on the plate. For a long minute he just stares at me and then he says, "Are you going to tell me how you came to have that much money?"

I look around and say, "I'd rather talk about that in private. Didn't mean to bring it up here, it just kind of slipped out."

Mark looks really uncomfortable for a second and then nods. "Okay, that makes sense. I hope it doesn't have anything to do with breaking any laws; that might put me in a difficult position."

"No," I say, "nothing like that. Can we eat now?"

I'm wishing I hadn't said anything about this. I thought that when you tell a preacher something it stays between the two of you. Maybe it would be better if I just took off tomorrow and forgot the rest of the stuff on my list.

I finish the chicken sandwich and fries and Mark eats most of his meal, and we both decide not to have dessert. Sandy is walking by and I say, "Hey, Sandy, can you add this up for us?"

"Sure," she says. "Separate checks?"

"No, just one," says Mark. "I've got this, Boone."

She nods and is gone for a minute, then comes back with a check and sets it on the table between us.

"I'll take care of that whenever you're ready," she says to me.

Mark reaches over and picks up the check. He looks at it and gets some bills out of his wallet and puts them on top of the check. He takes the pepper shaker and puts it on top and says, "You ready to go?"

He doesn't say much of anything on the way to the truck, or on the ride back to the home. I pull into a space and he says, "Nice truck. Quite an improvement over your last one. Would you like to come into my office and finish our conversation? I can promise you it's private."

We go in and sit down and I don't know what to say. Yesterday I was feeling all sorry for myself because of how Nancy hadn't introduced me to all her friends and here Mark gets treated like shit for no good reason, except I know that Daddy would have treated him the same way, and maybe I don't because I know him. I don't know.

I look up and Mark is studying me. "Forget about what happened at the restaurant, Boone. It's nothing, really. If I let that kind of sh—stuff bother me it would make me either crazy or angry all the time. Now, you said something about wanting Hannah to have a large amount of money that you tell me you came by honestly. Don't get all up in the air about this," he holds up his hand because he can see I don't like what he just said, "if you say it, I believe it. I have no reason not to. You have to admit, though, it's a little surprising."

I take a deep breath and start in, telling him about when Gamaliel had to go into the hospital, before he came to the home, and how he told me to keep his money for him and make sure Jerry never knew about it, and then later on when he told me that I should keep it hidden and how he wanted me to have it after he was gone, and how I put it in a safety deposit box at the bank and until I bought the truck the only thing I had spent any of it on was to get Frankie out of the vets, and how the reason I didn't spend any more than that was because it still felt like Gamaliel's money even though he's dead and I finally stop talking and I'm afraid to look up at Mark.

"Boone?"

I feel a hand on my shoulder.

"Boone?"

I'm still staring at the floor of Mark's office. There's tracks in the carpet where people have pushed chairs back and forth and a stain, something dark, I don't know what. It's old carpet, really old, and I think he ought to get some new carpet.

"Come on, Boone, look up. It's okay."

I straighten up and lean back in the chair. Mark goes back around his desk and sits down.

"Sorry," I say. "Once I got started talking I couldn't stop, I guess."

He looks at me without saying anything, and then he picks his hands up off the desk where they had been setting and spreads them wide. "You don't have anything to be sorry about, Boone," he says. "From what you said, you did exactly what Gamaliel wanted you to do. I think he would be fine with you doing what you want with the money. I did wonder about why you didn't tell Carrie after Gamaliel died, but since Jerry was still around, I can't fault you for that either."

"So what do I do about Hannah?" I ask him. "Now that you know all about this, how do I make sure that Hannah gets the money and not Aunt Claire?"

"You know," he says, "Claire is feeding and housing Hannah, and I don't — "

"That's between her and Momma," I interrupt him. "I never asked her to take off and leave me, or run to Claire and then dump Hannah the same way, or take up with that Jake asshole that tried to steal my old truck, or any of that. I can't take that on, Mark, she'll bleed me dry. You saw how she was, sitting right here in this office. She wouldn't lift a finger to find her own sister, tried to get me to do it for her. No, I'd like for Hannah to have something, but she's not going to be a grownup for a long time and I don't know how to do any of this."

"You'll have to give me some time to think about that," Mark says. "I feel like there should be a way, but I don't know what it might be."

I nod. I'm worn out, and it's only the middle of the afternoon. I was going to start packing for my trip and now all I want to do is go to sleep.

"Was there anything else?"

"I don't know what to do about Nancy, but to tell you the truth, Mark, I'm about done in. Maybe we could get together day after tomorrow?"

"Sure, sure we can. I'm going to be here all day. You just come by and if I'm with somebody, I'll make you next on the list. Okay?"

I go back to the house and take Frankie out on the leash, but I don't go up to where everybody is. I just want her to pee or whatever and go back in so I can have an S&S and lie down for a nap.

It's the middle of the night before I wake up, and then all I do is roll over and go back to sleep. When I wake up again it's early in the morning, earlier than

I've been up in a while. Frankie's nosing at me, which I guess is what woke me up. She's ready to go outside, so I get the leash and put my shoes on.

When we get back inside I look in the cabinets for something to eat and there's some dry cereal, but what I really want is something hot. I decide to go up and see if the cafeteria is open yet.

It is, and Melvin is going through the line. When he sees me he grabs his chest and staggers back against the counter like he's having a heart attack, and a couple of staff members run over to him and one of them has a walkie-talkie out, but he waves them off and says something and laughs, but they don't. They go off and he looks over at me and shrugs his shoulders, and then motions me to join him at his table. I get a tray and a plate full of eggs and biscuits and gravy and some hash browns and a cup of coffee and slide in opposite him.

"What in the world are you doing up at this hour, Boone? I thought you didn't get up until lunchtime."

He's having a really good time with this trip of mine. When I tell him I went to buy some supplies for it he asked me what I bought and said, "You need a good map book, that thing I gave you won't do more than get you started. There are so many side roads and little towns you'll need some kind of guide. Also, you need a leash that has a holder for dog poop bags."

I finish chewing what's in my mouth and then say, "What the hell did you just say?"

He laughs. "You will certainly need some way to dispose of Frankie's, uh, deposits when you take her out for a walk."

"You're kidding."

He grins at me. "Not kidding, Boone, some places have laws about it. You have to clean up after your dog. Throw it in a trash can."

"I'm supposed to pick up dog shit." This guy has to be lying to me.

"Well, not everywhere, but certainly in towns and cities. You can't just leave it there for somebody to step in. Next time you're out buying stuff for your trip look for pet leashes. Some of them will have little plastic containers full of small plastic bags. I'm not lying to you, Boone, I promise. Hey, Jasmine!"

The woman he shouted at comes over and he says, "Tell my young friend here that if he walks his dog in the city he'll have to pick up after her."

She nods. "It's true. And I appreciate it. I stepped in some once on the way to an appointment. Had to spend ten minutes in the bathroom cleaning my right shoe. Made me late."

Chapter Thirty-Nine

When I go to the bank and ask them what I do when I run out of checks, the woman I'm talking to says that nobody uses checks much anymore and that I ought to get a debit card. She explains about it and it sounds like a good idea, so I tell her to set it up. She says it'll take about three or four days before I get it, and I give her the address of the old folks home and tell her to send it there. I get another $600 out of the box and start to put it into my account and then I think they're going to start wondering where I got all this money, so I decide to just take it with me.

I spend the next three days getting the truck ready. Tiny looks it over again, even though he just did before I bought it, and says it all looks good.

"You'll need a set of rear tires in about 5,000 or 6,000 miles, but the front ones look good and so do the brakes. Have you tested the camper top yet?"

When I say no he goes into the shed and comes out with a water hose. "Climb on in there and make sure everything's closed up."

I do and in a second I hear water hitting the top of the camper. "Watch for leaks!" I hear Tiny's voice, and the spray moves all over the top and along both sides and the back.

When it stops I get out and say, "Nothing got in that I saw."

"Good deal. That'd be a nasty surprise."

After he finishes we sit and look at the truck and I say, "So are you coming?"

He looks down at the ground and then up at me. "I guess not, Boone. I got thinking about it and, well, I just can't do it. Not right now, anyways."

I don't say anything and after a minute he says, "It sure sounds like fun, though." After another minute he says, "You got balls, man, going off like that with the whole damn world in front of you."

Nobody's ever said anything like that to me, ever in my life.

"I need to write down your address so I can send you a card or something, tell you all about the fine looking women there are out there on the road."

He laughs. "You'll make me jealous." Then he looks at me. "You ever talk to Nancy? Speaking of fine looking women, that is."

"I tell you, man, I don't know what to do about that. I can't get within fifty feet of her, and I can't get her on the phone."

"So you plan to just take off without telling her? That's kind of cold, Boone. You sure there's no way to get to her?"

"Man, you think I want to go off and leave her? That girl's the best thing that ever happened to me and I know that, but her daddy's got her on such a short leash that I don't know if he's even going to let her go to college this fall or not. He's not kidding about this, Tiny. I mean, he's not."

"There's no reason to shout at me, you know." Tiny's not mad, as far as I can tell. He's just stating facts. "If you want me to, I can maybe get a letter or something to her. Or the number for that phone you just got. Might be after you're gone, it might take a while for her dad to calm down enough to back off, but if you wanted to leave something with me . . . ."

I don't say anything. I'm thinking, what would I say in a letter? I don't write stuff down, and this would be a really important letter. I probably need to, though, write a letter. Nancy and Hannah both.

Finally I look over at Tiny. "You know, for a stinking rich guy, you're all right."

He nods. "Thank you, Boone. And for poor white trash, you're not bad yourself."

I guess it's because I know him and we've been through a lot, but that doesn't even make me mad.

Something else occurs to me.

"You know, since you're going to stay here, I've got a bunch of shine I can't really take with me. I mean, since I'm underage and it's illegal to begin with, you know? You got a place you can store it in case I come back through sometime?"

"I might have to sample some every now and then," Tiny says, "but I can store it with what I've still got left. While we're talking about that, you think I could get a copy of Gamaliel's recipe? You know, in case I want to keep the tradition alive?"

The next day I take most of the shine and Gamaliel's old rifle up to Tiny's and give it all to him.

"I'll make a copy of the recipe and get that to you in a day or two."

"Sounds good," he says. "Nice rifle."

"I never fired it," I say, "so I don't know how nice it is. It's an old one that was in Gamaliel's toolshed."

"I might clean it up and test it out, if that's okay."

When I get back to the house I stand in the living room and look around. This is getting kind of scary, I guess because it looks like it might happen for real. I've got some of the stuff I need to start the trip, the rest of it I can pack in an hour or less, and this little house is not feeling much like home anymore. The cabinets are almost empty, and the fridge never had much in it to start with. I still need a cooler, I guess. I finger the safety deposit box key I've got hung around my neck and think I need to figure out how much I've got, get some to Hannah or leave it where Hannah can get to it, and try to figure out what to say to Nancy.

What I'd really like is to take off on this trip with her in the front seat with me and Frankie on one of those little kid seats in the back of the cab.

That's what I want to do, more than anything.

Chapter Forty

When I ask Betty if she's got a few minutes to talk, she says, "I was wondering when you'd get around to telling me you're leaving. That's what you want to talk about, isn't it?"

I'm not really surprised, because I figure Mark and Betty talk all the time, and I never told Mark to keep this a secret. At least I don't remember telling him that.

"Yeah, Betty, with Daddy and Momma both gone, and Gamaliel too, and Hannah's got Aunt Claire to watch out for her, seems like this would be a good time to get out of here."

She nods. "What did Nancy say when you told her?"

I don't say anything and she says, "You did tell her, right? For God's sake, Boone, you can't just run off and leave that girl. Don't you know how she feels about you?"

That makes me mad, and I try not to let it show but I'm not much good at that. "Listen, Betty, Nancy's dad won't let me or anybody else near her right now. Whatever happened, he's got that whole family locked up tight. I tried to see her, tried to call her, I don't know what else to do!"

She's got her back up now, I can tell. "Well, you just keep on trying then. You don't just run off like some kind of coward. Or don't you care anything about her?"

I take a step toward her and she backs up, and I can see she's scared. I turn around and head back down the hallway and she says, "Hold on there, young man! Don't you turn your back on me, not after all I've done for you!"

I don't even slow down. The door to the outside is on my left and I slam it open and almost hit one of the staff members. She's backing up to the door with somebody in a wheelchair and feeling behind her for the doorknob. By now I'm almost running and head back down to the house and start throwing stuff into boxes. I'm ready to leave right now.

There is an envelope on the kitchen counter that I guess Maryanne left here. It's addressed to me and it's from the bank. I open it and inside is the bank card and a note that tells me what my passcode is. 1881. I start to put it in my pocket with the card and then realize it's my age and my age backwards so I don't bother with the paper, just throw it and the envelope in the trash.

It's early afternoon and I was planning to go tell Melvin I was getting ready to leave, but I don't want to run into Betty, so I stay at the house. I don't like that much, though, because I really need to talk to Mark, see if he's figured out anything about Hannah. About the only thing I know to do right now is try to write Nancy something for Tiny to get to her after I'm already gone, so I sit down with a pen and paper I took from the dayroom up at the main building and try to figure out what to say.

Nancy,

If Tiny can get this to you maybe he'll have time to tell you that I'm gone. I can't stay around here anymore, everywhere I look reminds me of something bad. You're the only good thing, I know that much, and now I can't even see you.

I wish I'd had the chance to try some of that peach pie you made for my birthday. I bet it was real good, and I was too stupid to let you do that nice thing for me. Maybe one of these days.

I've got a cell phone now. The number is 555–197–1234. I'll try to remember to leave it turned on, so you can call me if you get a chance. I'll check in with Tiny every now and then and if he says things are okay I'll try to call you. I wish you were going with me. You're the best thing that ever happened to me, darlin'. In my whole life.

Boone

I read it over a couple of times; it's my fourth try and I don't like it much better than the other three, but I'm no damn good with words and never have been. Finally I give up and put it in an envelope and put her name on the outside.

There's two jars of the good stuff left and some of the regular shine in another jar. The rest is up at Tiny's. I pour the regular stuff into a glass and fill it up with Thunderstorm, and sit on the couch and drink it down slow.

After lunch the next day I take the letter up to Tiny, along with a copy of Gamaliel's recipe. He says if he can he'll get the letter to her. We both promise to call now and then.

I feel like I'm about done now.

When I get back to the home I go around to the side entrance and I'm about to go in when I hear Mark say, "Over here, Boone." I look around and he's sitting under the tree outside the chapel.

We sit and talk and I realize that I'm going to miss Mark a lot. He's a good man, even though Daddy used to say that preachers were all liars. Mark's not, and I don't have many friends but I think he is one.

I tell him I can't think what to say to Hannah in a letter and could he get my number to her and tell her to call me. I tell him I'll figure out something about the money while I'm gone and leave it in the bank for now, and he says that's good, because he hasn't been able to come up with anything. He says I need to tell all the old folks goodbye and let them say bye to Frankie, but I don't think I'm going to do that. I've got some paper left and I'll write Melvin a note and tell him I'll send him a postcard in a month or two. Now that I'm bound and determined to do this I can't stand to stay around here anymore.

The next morning I'm up early. I put the shotgun in the back of the truck under all my other stuff. I've thought off and on about getting rid of it because of Daddy, but I just can't seem to let it go for some reason. I get everything packed, including one jar of good stuff, and we head back to the main building. I have to make one more stop before I'm gone.

Mark's office is open but he's not in there, which is good. I put the keys to the little house in the middle of his desk along with the last jar of shine and a note.

Mark,

Remember Gamaliel when you sip on this. It's the last jar of his triple filtered shine and it is really smooth. He was one of the good guys, like you are. I'll call you sometime and let you know how things are going.

Boone

I don't know if he even drinks or not, but I feel like I ought to do something for him.

When we get to the road I turn right, because that's the way Nancy turned when we went to Knoxville that night. We're not on the road more than a minute when I see Mark's little car coming toward us. I roll down the window and wave when we pass him.

In the rear view mirror I can see his car pull over to the side of the road. Mark gets out and stands there beside it with his hand raised up high, watching us go. He gets a little smaller and then I top a rise and start down the other side and I can't see him any more.

End of Book Three